John Riddell

Mitre Court

A tale of the great city

John Riddell

Mitre Court
A tale of the great city

ISBN/EAN: 9783337121488

Printed in Europe, USA, Canada, Australia, Japan

Cover: Foto ©Andreas Hilbeck / pixelio.de

More available books at **www.hansebooks.com**

A Tale of the Great City.

BY

MRS. J. H. RIDDELL,

AUTHOR OF

"GEORGE GEITH OF FEN COURT," "SUSAN DRUMMOND,"

ETC.

IN THREE VOLUMES.

VOL. II.

LONDON :

RICHARD BENTLEY AND SON,

Publishers in Ordinary to Her Majesty the Queen.

1885.

CONTENTS OF VOL. II.

MITRE COURT.

CHAPTER I.

IN A CLEFT STICK.

MR. FRANK SCOTT, to quote John Jeffley's statement ● of the affair, "made off a sort of living" by sitting on a stool in a bill-discounter's office from nine in the morning till six o'clock at night.

This statement was not quite correct, because young Scott's stool chanced frequently to be vacant, while the clerk himself was running about London on his employer's business, and his hours were often longer than those mentioned. Still, the main facts were beyond dispute. To Mr. Jeffley's influence

Frank Scott owed his appointment, and he was very thankful to have secured it.

When first he entered Fowkes' Buildings, he felt friendless and desolate, as a stranger can feel only in a great city. He had just come from the Mediterranean, and the captain of the vessel, in which he chanced to be the only passenger, recommended him so strongly to put up at Mrs. Jeffley's, that though the young fellow hesitated about the matter, he allowed himself to be over-persuaded, and permitted his new friend to take him in tow, and pilot the Scott craft safe into that still anchorage, lying as within a snug breakwater just out of the roar and bustle of Great Tower Street.

Mrs. Jeffley did not much approve of this new inmate. The captain who performed that necessary ceremony of introduction was a person who had never stood very high in her good books. Some misunderstanding about a gallon of Scotch whisky, which had been consumed by a favourite lodger, while paid for by the captain, had caused a reference to Mr. Jeffley; which Mrs. Jeffley regarded, and rightly, as an infringement of her prerogative as master of the house.

Jack, in his " stupid way," at once gave his verdict in favour of the captain, a " mean, suspicious wretch nobody wanted to cheat, or thought of cheating." For a long time after that, Mrs. Jeffley felt all her rose-leaves were crumpled.

" The idea," she said, " of making such a fuss about nothing ; and going to Mr. Jeffley, too, when a fresh gallon was offered as fair and handsome as possible."

Over that matter the shoe pinched horribly. If honest Jack were innocent of knowledge concerning many things, he at least understood the difference between an old and a new whisky, and gave judgment accordingly in favour of the gentleman whose liquor had been consumed without his leave.

For this reason Mrs. Jeffley never subsequently looked with much favour on young Scott's friend.

" Yes, he can have a room," she said, answering the inquiry as to whether the captain's companion might tell the cabman to fetch in his luggage. "As you know, I do not care to take in people unable to give my price; still, as you tell me he won't give trouble, and means to pay his way regularly, I'll see what I can do."

It was not a gracious permission, or graciously spoken. Nevertheless, the weary young man felt glad to avail himself of it.

Ere many days were over, he and Mr. Jeffley happening to meet on the threshold, spoke; and Jack "took to him."

Again they spoke, and Jack took to him more; took to him with special liking, because the youth said "he was tired of living among foreigners, would prefer a crust in England to a whole kid out there," meaning those distant lands, the inhabitants of which Mr. Jeffley hated more than, he confessed, it becomes any Christian to hate anybody, even "though he be a Papist," finished Jack, whose religious ideas were as mixed as his notions of geography.

"He's one of the right sort," said Mr. Jeffley to the acquaintance whose good services he chanced to be entreating on

behalf of Frank Scott. " I won't tell you
he's very bright, because I don't know that
he is ; but his head's screwed on the right
way, and he'll be honest and painstaking,
I'll go bail."

It was in consequence of this temperate
eulogium that place in the bill-broker's came
to be secured.

" I'd rather you were going anywhere else,"
remarked Mr. Jeffley, whose conception of
the business of a bill-broker was crude in the
extreme. His people had never had to do
with such folks, and it is to be feared Jack
imagined young Scott's employer was but a
richer sort of bailiff.

" Likely as not a money-lender—sixty per
cent. chap," which, indeed, the wealthy and
respectable individual through whose hands
millions per annum passed was not.

His white hair would have stood on end
had anyone brought such business to him.

Queer paper, nevertheless, did find its way
sometimes into Mr. Brintolf's office, No. 133,
Birchin Lane—very queer—which it is but
simple justice to say Mr. Brintolf only dis-

counted because of the firms through whose instrumentality he made its acquaintance.

Running brokers, too, brought strange documents thither, which sometimes were "put through," and sometimes not. Often the running broker's commission was of the smallest. Often, too, Mr. Brintolf, talking to his right-hand man, remarked : "We cannot have any more of this sort of thing ;" or, " Really, Mr.—— ought to know better."

In such an office, of necessity little passes but what is known to the clerks.

Mere machines they may seem to an outsider, or even to their principal—mere calculating figures, mere writing, copying, carrying machines ; but for all that, neither deaf nor blind.

They may not have much money in their pockets, but they carry weighty knowledge in their heads. They know the needy man, though his coat may be glossy, his hat new, his linen spotless, and his manner jaunty ; credit at his tailor's and unlimited impudence do not deceive them. It is as well known in the office whether from that inner room a man passes out empty or full, as whether the bills of some great firm have been duly paid or returned dishonoured.

Often their information is fuller and more accurate than that of their employer. They are out and about—they hear words dropped that grow weighty when attached to other words ; without a syllable being uttered they read the meaning of a " reference" or a look. They know all the delicate shades of mean- ing attached to such phrases as " refer to drawer," " cheques not cleared," " will be attended to," and so forth.

The writing on the wall was no plainer to Daniel than the story to which the notary's legend may in business be said to form chapter one of volume three.

All these things and many more became familiar as the alphabet to Frank Scott before he had been in Mr. Brintolf's service six months ; what he never, however, could understand, was how his principal permitted himself to lose, for the sake of an eighth or even sixteenth per cent., thousands.

Often firms known to the profane outer world as "shaky," whose paper was freely spoken of as "fishy," could get discount almost up to the hour of final suspension.

"I would not do it," thought Frank, criticising, as is the manner of clerks, his employer's mode of doing business.

No doubt Mr. Scott thought himself very wise in his generation — probably he was wise; yet the fact remains that Mr. Brintolf continued rich, and Frank stayed poor.

Once in his zeal the young man ventured to give his principal a hint that there were rumours floating about the solvency of a certain house; but he was met with such a snub, he retired from the interview crestfallen.

"You'll perhaps keep a quiet tongue in your head for the future," sneered one of his fellows; and he was so far right that if Mr. Frank Scott had heard on good authority the Bank of England was going to suspend payment, he would have uttered no warning note to Mr. Brintolf.

"I wish you were out of it," said Mr. Jeffley more than once, but his protégé did not make any complaint. He was an assiduous worker, always ready, always willing, always punctual, always well. If he found it sometimes hard work to make both ends meet, he did not say so. Thanks to the kindness and favour of Mr. Jeffley, he enjoyed many advantages at Fowkes' Buildings. He was made free of the Sunday dinner at a mere nominal charge; as a guest he often supped in Jack's sanctum; he shared the master's fire, and Mr. Jeffley had always a kind look and cheering word for him—both of which were far more to the lonely young fellow's heart than the various material advantages he enjoyed through his friend's favour.

Mrs. Jeffley was not always, as has been hinted, considerate to him, on occasion using her lodger, who had so little money to spare, almost scurvily, and certainly grudging the liking that unworthy creature Jack entertained for a person who had come, nobody knew from where; but all this did not ruffle

Frank's composure much, or affect Jack Jeffley at all.

"The lad has more packed away inside him than many people think for," he was wont to remark in his "slow" thoughtful manner. "He has more in him than *I* gave him credit for."

"Pity he does not turn to and make something out of it," retorted Mrs. Jeffley. "Why, as Mr. Katzen truly says, he's only earning boy's wages and doing man's work."

"That's right enough," returned Mr. Jeffley, though not cordially, for he did not like admitting that Mr. Katzen could be right, even in so self-evident a matter.

"And why he refused such a good offer as Mr. Katzen made him I am sure I can't imagine."

Mr. Jeffley thought he could, but he was wise enough to hold his tongue.

"But there, I suppose he knows his own business best," proceeded Mrs. Jeffley.

"I dare say he does," agreed Mr. Jeffley meekly.

" Or *thinks* he does," snapped Mrs. Jeffley.

" He tells me he is gaining great experience," ventured Jack.

" It is to be hoped it will do him some good," said Mrs. Jeffley.

" I am sure I hope it will," answered her husband.

" And I am very sure it won't," retorted Mrs. Jeffley.

" I think you are wrong, my dear."

" Time will show," was the reply. " Here he is, though, and I suppose wanting his tea, just as if he paid me thousands a year instead of a few shillings a week."

" A man wants his tea whether he's rich or poor," declared Mr. Jeffley, which suggestion being only received with a disgusted " There ! get out of my way, do. Can't you see I want to open the sideboard ?" Jack repaired to a window that presented a view over nothing, and fell to whistling softly.

In the middle of this performance Frank Scott entered the room. As matters turned out, he did not desire any tea—all he wished was Mr. Jeffley's companionship to the theatre.

Two tickets had been given him, and he proposed they should repair to the Adelphi together.

Mr. Jeffley, however, refused to avail himself of the chance. He was tired, he said, and too old to care for such things. If the Missis liked to go with Frank——

" The Missis has something else to do," interrupted Mrs. Jeffley.

" Then perhaps some one in the house may care for the tickets," said Frank, laying them on the table; " I won't go if you or Mr. Jeffley don't."

" Well, I'm sure!" declared Mrs. Jeffley, but what she was sure of she never condescended to explain.

" Come out for a stroll, Mr. Jeffley, as you won't go to the theatre," entreated Frank; " it's a lovely evening, and a stroll will do you good."

" Well, I don't mind if I do stretch my legs a bit," conceded Mr. Jeffley, moving lazily towards the door.

" They're too long already," remarked his better half, unconsciously repeating an old joke, which, however, she did not mean for a joke. To her the whole business of her husband's misdeeds seemed most serious.

"You need not be afraid ; they'll not grow much more, mother, I think," said Mr. Jeffley with a deprecatory laugh. "Come along, Frank!" And the pair departed, pursued by a shrill aspiration from Mrs. Jeffley that she hoped they'd get "home before morning."

"Which way ?" asked Mr. Jeffley, as they emerged into Great Tower Street.

"Any way that is quiet," answered Frank, "for I have something particular to say to you."

"Let's take a turn, then, through Finsbury. The Circus is quiet enough at all times. Nothing gone wrong at the office, I hope ?"

"Nothing at all. The matter I want to talk to you about does not concern me, except indirectly, in the least."

"All right, then," exclaimed Mr. Jeffley cheerfully; "now I can wait with an easy mind till you like to begin."

They were about to cross the street at Mark Lane, when they met Abigail walking swiftly eastward. Mr. Jeffley lifted his hat, but Frank took no notice of her, while she looked at him as she might at a stranger.

"Likely girl, that," remarked Mr. Jeffley, turning his head and looking after the retreating figure. "You know who she is, I suppose?"

"Mr. Brisco's ward, isn't she?"

"Yes, that is so. Hillo! there's Katzen— see him?"

Frank Scott did see that gentleman scudding rapidly along in the direction Abigail had just taken. For a second he turned red and hesitated; then, setting his face steadily northward, he said:

"If we stop looking after everyone we know, we shan't get to Finsbury to-night."

In the City, business was over for the day. The lanes, streets, and alleys lately teeming with anxious hurrying life were lone and silent as some country road. The men who had a few hours before hurried through them, intent on improving the last commercial moment that day might hold, were scattered north, east, south, and west. They were

dressing for dinner in Belgravia ; they had
partaken of tea at Bow ; some—care keeping them close company—sauntered through
well-kept grounds at Dulwich, Herne Hill,
Beckenham, and other favourite resorts close
to the People's Palace ; out Enfield and Bar-
net very many resorted, thankful for the keen,
bracing air which seemed to string up their
nerves for another wrestle with fate ; wherever they were scattered these City bees—at
all events they had left for a time the great
hive empty. To a few housekeepers, companies' porters, beadles, the members of the
Fire Brigade, small retail shopkeepers, the
care of the deserted City was entrusted.

Children skipped on the pavement ; women,
nursing their babies, stood in the doorways, or
sat on the steps ; Italians ground out popular
airs on asthmatic organs, while little girls
danced and little boys gaped. The silent
hour held its spell over that small, surprisingly
rich, immensely powerful land guarded by
a mythical dragon, and a scarce more real
grasshopper. Anyone who liked to talk
might have done so to his heart's content.

"What is hindering you?" asked Mr. Jeffley. "We are quiet enough now in all conscience."

"Wait a minute," said Frank; "I think I shall be able to talk better in the Circus.

They turned along New Broad Street and walked on in silence till they had passed Moorfields Chapel and were close to the London Institution, then the younger man slipped his hand within Jack's arm. What a brawny arm it was!—what a stalwart fellow! Upright in mind and body, Frank felt his friend to be.

"Well, old boy?" said Jack interrogatively, but Frank only drew a little nearer to his side—a little nearer still.

"Doesn't this suit you?" asked Mr. Jeffley. "Why, you must be hard to please. Come —out with whatever it is you have in your mind. Screw up your courage. Like a bad tooth—one wrench, and it will be over."

Frank laughed.

"I am going to ask you something," he said. "You must not be offended."

"Go ahead—it's not easy to offend me."

" I only want to know if your people have
latterly found their business falling off at
all ?"

Jack Jeffley stopped short.

" What the —— concern is that of yours ?"
he retorted.

The expression Jack used was very strong
indeed, for he felt both surprised and
angry.

" Do not eat me up alive before I have
said what I want to say," entreated the other.
" Why can't you give me a straight answer
to a straight question ? I did not ask it out
of mere curiosity, believe me."

" I don't care what the deuce you asked it
out of," returned Mr. Jeffley. " If you think
you are going to get me to talk about the
affairs of my employers you are confoundedly
mistaken—that's all !"

" Then you won't tell me ? No, you need
not try to throw me off, for I have a great
deal to tell you——"

" Have you ? And suppose I don't want
to hear it ?"

" I intend that you shall hear it. Come,

Mr. Jeffley, hasn't trade been somewhat dull lately ?"

" Now look here," said the person thus addressed, stopping suddenly in the middle of the pavement, and surveying his companion with eyes full of amazed and sad rebuke. " I don't want to quarrel with you, but I must if you go on in this way. When I first went to Deedes I said to myself, ' Now, Jack, you must mind what you're about. Talk as much as you like about your own affairs, but no talk, if you please, concerning your masters'. Whether they are doing well or ill, say nothing. Turn the key on your mouth as you do on the cellars.' I have done that during all the years I've been with them. No man, or woman either, has known aught of Deedes' business through me. What I've never mentioned to my own wife it's unlikely I'd speak about to a stripling like yourself, so drop it—that's all I've to say. One word's as good as ten when a man's in earnest. Drop it, or I'll have to drop you."

" No, Mr. Jeffley, you won't," replied

Frank; "not even when I tell you that without word from you I know Deedes' business has been falling off. No—I shall not stop now till I have finished my say. You 'can't think where the trade is going.' Messrs. Deedes don't know where the trade has gone, but I know. Mr. Gregson, though drawing a salary from your house, is working a business on his own account, and if your people do not put a spoke in his wheel, they will soon find themselves without custom— that's all."

As Frank Scott proceeded in his sentence Mr. Jeffley's face was a study. Horror and incredulity were stamped upon it, and for a moment after the stream of information ceased to inundate him, he remained silent, like one suddenly stricken dumb.

"Repeat that all again, will you?" he said at last; "it's a good joke, I dare say, but I scarcely grasp the full beauty of it yet. I never was, to say, very quick."

"There is not much of joke about the matter," answered Frank. "Your manager has been skimming the cream of your trade

for many a month past. If that is a jest, I
cannot see it."

"Get along with you, do!" exclaimed Mr.
Jeffley, giving the young man a playful
shove. "For a minute you frightened me—
made my heart leap into my mouth—but I
know you are only making fun. Mr. Gregson a rogue—why, you will be saying next I
have been robbing the firm!"

"No, I will not; but I know and will stick
to what I say, that Mr. Gregson is carrying
on a business in King Street, Piccadilly,
under another name, and that he is gradually
working up a connection there."

"Oh! this is going a trifle too far," said
Mr. Jeffley, laughing uneasily. "Perhaps as
you have told me so much, you won't mind
adding the name he trades under?"

"I was going to tell you that. He is
associated with Rothsattel and Co., who are
considered to import the finest Rhenish and
Moselle wines that find their way into
London."

"Rothsattel and Co.!" repeated Jack Jeffley,
stunned.

"Yes, they have offices in King Street;
one restaurant in Crown Court; another
just out of Leicester Square; and a third
in Paul's Bakehouse Yard, Godliman
Street."

"Do you know what you are saying?"
asked Mr. Jeffley.

"Certainly I do. I can give you chapter
and verse for every statement I have advanced. Mr. Gregson is selling some of your
firm's old port and special sherries in order
to attract custom, but before long he will be
strong enough to kick St. Dunstan's Hill
over; and when he does, if Messrs. Deedes
let him go on long enough, they may look
out—that is all."

"But how did you come to an understanding of all this?" asked Mr. Jeffley.

"By keeping my mouth shut and my eyes
and ears open," answered Frank shortly. "I
have had my suspicions for a long time; but
I would not speak till I had proof positive.
As sure as I stand here Mr. Gregson is
underselling you, and sending your customers
to Rothsattel, where they can get such hock

and claret as cannot be had except for fabulous prices elsewhere."

" I don't believe it," said Mr. Jeffley. " I do not mean that I think you are inventing the story, but you are deceived, that is all. You are mistaken—totally——"

"Am I ? Oh ! very well—perhaps I may be—only let there be no mistake on one point. Do not forget I have warned you in time ; and when the worst comes, hold me blameless."

" Wait a minute, wait a minute, don't be in such a hurry. Can you wonder at my being loth to take in a story like this all at once ? It is not easy to gulp it down. Though I never was over and above partial to Mr. Gregson, still, you know, this goes beyond everything. It is impossible to credit that a man of his character and holding his position could turn out such a blackguard."

" I do not ask you to credit what I have taken a lot of time to find out, but I am ready to stand to it anywhere and before any one. Tell your people or not, just as you like. The matter does not concern me, but I have a shrewd suspicion you will find it affect you."

"Dear—dear," said Mr. Jeffley piteously, "what a hot-headed chap you are! You first take my breath away, and then you abuse me like a pickpocket, because I can't see as you do. Here's a nice cleft stick you put me in. There never was a fellow hated mischief-making and story-telling more than I do. I've tried to steer a clear course—to keep out of trouble and make none. With what sort of a face could I go before my gentlemen and say, 'Mr. Gregson, while pocketing your money, is slyly cutting your throat'? They would think I was mad, and send for a police-man and a strait-waistcoat."

"I have no doubt they would," replied young Scott, "if you spoke as you speak to me, and looked as you are looking now! Better consider what I have told you, and what I can prove; but I warn you there is no time to lose. Take your courage in your hand about ten o'clock to-morrow, and let your firm know how the case stands. Sup-posing they want me, send a line to Birchin

Lane, and I'll run round in the middle of the day."

"See, Scott," began Mr. Jeffley, "do you mean this seriously ; do you say, *upon your soul,* what you have told me is all gospel truth—that you think it is my bounden duty to let the people I serve know they are being cheated ?"

"Upon my soul, I have told you nothing but what is the bare truth, and if you do not let your people know at once you will repent your silence."

There ensued a moment of irresolution ; then in the twilight Frank could see his friend's countenance hardening into determination.

"I won't sleep on it," he said at last. "Come along with me (you'll face it out too, won't you ?) to Mr. Fulmer ; he lives with his mother in Hamilton Place, close by Hyde Park Corner. We'll take a Piccadilly 'bus at the Bank. You make no objection, I suppose?"

"I make no objection," answered the younger man ; "that which I have said I will stick to."

CHAPTER II.

R. FULMER proved to be at home, and on sending in their names Jack and his friend were ushered into a library, where, so said the servant, his master would soon see them.

Jack sat down near the door. Frank took a chair at a little distance. Neither addressed a word to the other; since leaving Finsbury Circus they had not spoken a syllable. When young Scott would have settled the fare, Mr. Jeffley, with a mute gesture, signified that he meant to be paymaster. Had both men been going to execution they could not have showed a graver or steadier front. Had Jack repaired to Hamilton Place to confess that since his first entry into Messrs. Deedes' service his life could not be regarded save as a long fraud, his face could scarcely have seemed sadder, or his manner been more overstrung. Great emotions were in fact things quite out of his line. He would have made a wretched tragedian. To his simple mind it appeared horrible that wickedness could exist at all; but that it should enter even into that holy of holies, Deedes' offices, and in the shape of a trusted and confidential servant, appeared worse still. Further, he did not feel at all satisfied as to how Mr. Fulmer might receive his communication. He had doubts about Frank Scott, just as the Israelites had when they saw David starting to meet the Philistine with naught in his hand save a sling and five smooth stones. He believed the young fellow was confident of the righteousness of his case; but Mr. Fulmer might not see with his eyes, or hear with his ears, and if he failed to do so, Jack did not of course know exactly what might come to pass. Only he thought storms would ensue—storms and tempests likely to render Deedes' cellars anything rather than safe or pleasant places in which to remain.

However, if a thing had to be done, the sooner it was done the better. Jack felt that after such a communication he could not have closed his eyes the whole night long.

If the story were a mistake—why, Mr. Fulmer was the proper person to satisfy himself on that point. To Jack Jeffley's possibly dull mind there seemed to be but one course to take, and so he took it. Supposing it necessary to open such a dreadful budget, nothing could be gained by deferring the operation till the next morning. For good or for evil he would get the affair over ; and having thus determined, he sat silent, while Frank Scott sat silent too.

On the mantelpiece a clock ticked softly. It chimed three-quarters past eight o'clock, then four. While the last stroke of nine was sounding, the door opened and Mr. Fulmer came in. He was a large man, taller than Mr. Jeffley, and about twice his girth. He had a bull neck, a broad forehead, grizzly black hair, which had already served its

owner the scurvy trick of leaving him partly
bald ; shaggy eyebrows ; dark, not unkindly
eyes ; a short nose inclined to turn up ; a
large mouth destitute of corners ; a great
expanse of closely shaved chin—an even
greater expanse of face destitute of any
natural ornament save a bristling, greyish
moustache ; not an atom of breed in a single
feature, though his mother was an earl's
daughter, but yet with a certain look of
power about him inherited possibly from the
paternal Fulmer, who had left enough money
behind him to render his son a very important
partner in the St. Dunstan Hill firm.

His garments fitted him as tightly as clothes
could do. The tailor's skill must have been
put on its mettle to compass such a miracle
of bracing-in.

Both men rose at his entrance.

" Be seated—be seated," he said with a
lordly air. " Sorry to have kept you waiting.
Jeffley, but I was at dinner. What is it ?—
warehouse not on fire, I hope ?"

" No, the warehouse is not on fire, sir ; at
least it was not when I saw it last. I have

come about a worse matter than fire, I am afraid."

"Worse matter than fire!" repeated Mr. Fulmer. "Why, what could be worse? Mr. Deedes is not dead, is he?"

"Not that I am aware of, sir. The fact is——" but here Jack broke down abruptly and looked appealingly towards Frank Scott.

"What is the fact?" asked Mr. Fulmer, glancing impatiently from one to the other of his visitors. "If you are aware of the nature of what Mr. Jeffley has come to say," he added, speaking direct to Frank Scott, "help him out, will you? Don't let us keep the matter dawdling about all the evening."

"Mr. Jeffley wants to tell you something concerning your manager, which he thinks it behoves you to know," answered the younger man thus appealed to.

"About Gregson? He has not bolted, has he?"

"No, he has not bolted," answered Mr. Jeffley, adopting for convenience' sake his principal's unconventional expression, and indeed too dazed to know well what he was saying ; " but I hear he is working a business on his own account, and——"

" Stop a moment," commanded Mr. Fulmer. " When did you hear this ?"

" To-night, sir ; an hour ago."

" How did you hear it ?"

" He heard it from me," said Frank Scott boldly.

" This is a very serious charge," observed Mr. Fulmer. " I hope you are prepared to substantiate it ?"

" I think I can substantiate it," answered the young man with modest assurance. But to Jack Jeffley that word " think " sounded like the knell of doom.

" You shall tell me the story your own way," observed Mr. Fulmer, in that quiet tone which conveyed such an idea of power ; " but first I wish to know who you are."

" My name is Francis Scott," was the reply. " I am clerk in Mr. Brintolf's office in Birchin Lane, and I lodge with Mr. Jeffley."

" What is Mr. Brintolf ?"

" A bill-broker."

" Very good ; now go on."

Frank Scott went on.   He told how, being on one occasion instructed to call and order some Rhenish wine for Mr. Brintolf from Messrs. Rothsattel and Co., the invoice was made out for him by Mr. Gregson, whom he knew by sight.

" I thought that odd," proceeded the young man, "but the matter slipped from my memory till I had occasion to go to Roth-sattels' again.   That time I did not see Mr. Gregson, but I heard his voice in the counting-house.   He and Mr. Conrad Roth-sattel—as I learnt afterwards the younger Mr. Rothsattel is called—were talking in German.   I understand German, and as they were not speaking in whispers, I soon gathered Mr. Gregson had a large stake in the King Street business.   Then it occurred to me something strange must be going on, because I could not imagine it likely you would give your consent to such an arrange-ment.   Still, in London one never knows. After a while, however, two of Mr. Brintolf's customers began to talk in our office about

the quality of Rothsattels' wines. One said
they were selling wonderfully fine ports and
sherries at a comparatively low rate; the
other said he had dealt with you for years,
and defied any firm in London to beat you in
quality; his friend laughed, and advised him
to give Rothsattels' a trial. They got their
Spanish wines, he assured the other, from
the same house as supplied you, and yet they
sold the same or a superior article at five-
and-twenty per cent. less. The very next
day I saw your van delivering wine at Rothsattels' place in Leicester Square. Then I
began to get uneasy, and thought I would
devote myself a little to finding out the rights
of the matter."

"And you discovered——"

"That Mr. Gregson is drawing on Rothsattel and Co., and Rothsattel and Co. are
drawing on Gregson; that they are both
paying pretty high for having their paper
done—that when any of your customers want,
say, a fine Moselle wine, Mr. Gregson
remarks, 'You had better go to Rothsattels'
in King Street, Piccadilly, our firm never

touch those light wines.' Then when the man goes to King Street he is asked to taste one of your own sherries, and told he can be supplied at some low figure. Of course the object is to work up a trade. Almost any day Mr. Gregson may announce his intention of leaving you, but meantime he is doing you all the injury he possibly can."

" It sounds ingenious—and there may be something in what you suggest," observed Mr. Fulmer. " May I ask how you came to be cognizant of that little matter of the cross bills ? Through your employer's books, eh ?"

" No," answered Frank, colouring a little. " Mr. Brintolf has never, so far as I am aware, had any other dealings with Roth-sattel or Gregson than purchasing a few dozens of Nierstein, for which his son, who is delicate, has a fancy."

" Then how did you get to know so much about this affair ?"

" I would rather not tell you, because the person who mentioned these bills to me might get into trouble. He spoke casually on the subject—quite accidentally. He did not know at the time I had any interest in the people, and he does not know now."

"You have busied yourself considerably to get at all these details."

"Yes, I suppose I have."

"And what do you expect to receive in return ?"

"I am afraid I do not exactly understand."

"For so clever a young fellow you have become suddenly rather stupid. Indeed, I am inclined to believe you are somewhat stupid—you ought to have bargained for your price beforehand."

"I have no price."

"Leave your reward to our generosity—eh ? Surely that was scarcely wise ?"

"I want no reward."

"You mean to tell me you have taken all this extraordinary amount of trouble out of pure consideration for, and a friendly feeling towards, our firm ?"

"I do not mean to tell you anything of the kind," retorted Frank. "If Mr. Jeffley had not chanced to be in your employment, Mr. Gregson might have gone on playing his double game for ever without let or hindrance from me."

" You do not consider it your duty then to expose villainy ?"

" Indeed I do not. I have something else to think of than stripping the masks off rogues I meet every day of my life. Further, Mr. Fulmer, if you will forgive a young man poor as I am speaking so bluntly to a man rich as you are—I have a notion that great firms ought to be able to find out for themselves whether they are being cheated without any help or private information from outsiders."

" Frank, I never thought you would let your tongue run away with you," remonstrated Mr. Jeffley.

" If I have said anything to offend Mr. Fulmer, I beg to apologize," answered the young man. " What I did, I did for you, and you only. Perhaps I had better have held my peace and let Mr. Gregson run to the end of his tether. However, that can't be helped now."

" You are a very hot-tempered young

man," remarked Mr. Fulmer, with an indulgent smile.

" Perhaps you are right," answered Frank, " though no one ever accused me of being so before this evening."

" I assure you, sir, that is quite true," pleaded Mr. Jeffley ; "long as I have known Scott, he has never in my presence lost his self-control till now."

" Which only shows how true it is, we may live with a person for years and have no idea of his real character," said Mr. Fulmer enigmatically.

" Having heard what I did hear," observed Mr. Jeffley, reverting to the original question, " I thought it only my duty to come straight away to you, sir."

" *That* I quite understand," answered Mr. Fulmer. " What I do *not* understand, however, is why your friend here considered it *his* duty to stir in the matter."

" As I have said before, no feeling of duty entered into the question," retorted Frank. " Mr. Jeffley has shown kindness to me ever since I first saw him, and I thought—erroneously it seems—that, as a matter of common gratitude, I ought to let him know there was an unprincipled scoundrel in the same employment as himself."

"You have done no harm by your interference as yet," remarked Mr. Fulmer, with calm tolerance. "If you can manage to say nothing more, you may perhaps do good."

"You may rest satisfied I shall meddle no further in the matter," said Frank, with conviction.

He had risen some time previously in order to deliver his sentiments with greater effect, and as the conversation proceeded, Mr. Jeffley had risen likewise in order to keep him company.

"If you had not so explicitly stated you were only desirous of serving Mr. Jeffley," observed Mr. Fulmer, also rising as if to end the interview, "I would thank you for your well-meant warning."

"No need to thank me," muttered the young man, moving towards the door.

"Good-night," said Mr. Fulmer civilly; "I am afraid you have given yourself a vast

amount of trouble. Good-night, Mr. Jeffley.
I shall see you in the morning."

" I hope to the Lord," thought Jack as he
strode along Piccadilly, experiencing some
difficulty in keeping pace with Frank's impatient steps, " he has not it in his mind to
give *me* notice. I should scarce feel a bit
surprised ; and Mr. Deedes ill too, and Mr.
Tunstall trying to break his neck in Switzerland. Do you know," he said, not angrily
or nastily, because that was not Jack's way,
but with a sort of mild expostulation, " I
cannot see why we should walk so *very* fast,
even though Mr. Fulmer did chance to rile
you."

"Oh! I am not riled," answered Frank,
slackening his pace, however ; " still, he is a
beast."

"Come, come, gently now," said Mr.
Jeffley, as though soothing a restive horse.
" Mr. Fulmer is not half a bad fellow, if you
know how to take him. Every man has his
own ways, and people like ourselves have to
put up with them. I found it hard at first to
remember my right place ; but bless you,

that's nothing to fret about when you get used to it. I suppose you did not give the matter a thought, but first or last you never once said ' sir ' to him."

" Who is he that I should ' sir ' him ?" asked Frank hotly. " He is not my master."

" He is mine, though," answered Jack.

" If I have done you any harm with him," exclaimed the young man, instantly penitent, " I am sorry ; but he did provoke me. From the first he looked and spoke as if we were both dirt under his feet ; and then to ask me what I expected for trying to do his firm a good turn. Confound him !"

" I hope you feel better now," suggested Mr. Jeffley.

" I only wish," went on Frank, " I had never opened my lips about the matter."

" So don't I," returned his friend. " It was right for my people to know what is going on. Whatever happens, I shall be glad to think you told them. It is off our shoulders now. Come, cheer up !"

It was impossible to resist Mr. Jeffley's honest face and hearty manner, and after a

little Frank did try to cheer up and strive to
master his irritation. Notwithstanding his
best efforts, however, he carried a somewhat
gloomy face back with him to Fowkes'
Buildings ; while Jack, over whom the idea
of losing his post loomed darkly, played so
indifferent a part at supper that Mrs. Jeffley
exclaimed in hot indignation :

" I wonder what has come to all you
men to-night. There's Mr. Katzen taken
himself off to bed in a tantrum about something or other, and now here you come in
looking as pleasant as if you had found
sixpence and lost a shilling."

" You must not be cross with me, wifey, if
I am not very bright," answered Jack, getting
up and stroking the divine Maria's still
abundant hair. " We have walked rather
too far, and I feel done up a trifle—that's
all."

" And enough too," remarked Mrs. Jeffley,
" when it makes you look as if everybody
belonging to you was dead and buried."

" I ought not to have persisted in walking
back," said Frank. " It is all my fault, Mrs.

Jeffley ; and I am now so tired myself I think the best thing I can do is to follow Mr. Katzen's example and go to bed."

" And I'll do the same thing," declared Mr. Jeffley, adding softly as he and Frank passed up the stairs together, " I wonder what has put Katzen out ?"

Miss Abigail's lover, had he chosen, could have hazarded a guess on the subject.

In no worse temper perhaps had Mr. Katzen ever returned to the Jeffley mansion. Abigail contrived to give him the slip in Great Tower Street, but calling subsequently in Botolph Lane, he secured the doubtful advantage of half an hour's *tête-à-tête* with his lady-love.

He found her not in the least changed for the better. She flouted, derided, tormented him. Of her own accord she said she had met with a gentleman who was going to teach her the organ.

" Young or old ?" questioned Mr. Katzen.

" Young, of course," she replied, "but a great musician. He studied in Germany, and is steeped in harmony up to his very ears."

"I suppose that is why you are learning German," Mr. Katzen observed.

"Perhaps," she answered, without expressing surprise at his knowledge.

"So as to be able to talk with him in that language?"

"Yes—and unless you are present, no one will know what we are saying. We can say anything we like then."

"It seems to me you make no scruple about saying anything you like in English."

"Oh! I don't know—a foreign tongue seems to give one such freedom."

"Well, I wish you joy of your freedom with your new friend—or shall I say lover?"

"You can say which you like." Not exactly an agreeable permission.

Mrs. Jeffley was quite right—something had "come to" her mankind that evening.

Jack tossed and tumbled through the hours which should have been devoted to sleep, dreading the interview indicated by Mr. Fulmer as impending, yet heartily wishing it over.

About noon next day that gentleman made

his appearance at the vaults, ostensibly to issue directions concerning some wine lying in bond, but really to remark to Mr. Jeffley :

" It will be as well to say nothing about the matter we were speaking of last night. Your irascible young friend may be mistaken, or he may have exaggerated matters a little. In any case I wish no notice taken of the affair. You understand me ?"

Jack did not in the least, though he answered " Perfectly, sir."

" And if you see your friend you might give him a hint."

" He won't need one, sir; but I will tell him what you say."

" Thank you, Jeffley. Things are very quiet."

" Very quiet indeed, sir ; but they are always quiet at this time of the year."

CHAPTER III.

MR. GREGSON.

SAVE that Mr. Fulmer—who had never previously been in the habit of visiting those dim vaults where so much wealth was placed under the hand of Mrs. Jeffley's husband—suddenly seemed to have taken a fancy for intruding at strange and unexpected hours on a territory Jack felt to be almost a possession of his own, things —after that interview in Hamilton Place— went on much as they had done before Frank and his friend wended their way westward.

So far as Mr. Gregson was concerned, Jack decided, no warning might ever have been uttered.

"I knew how it would be," he thought.

" Still, as the young chap thought he saw smoke, I suppose it was right for him to shout ' Fire !' It appears there was no fire after all ; still, there might have been. All the same, I wish he had held his tongue. It's not over-pleasant, after so many years of honest hard service, to find a master taking it into his head to suspect *me* of not being quite on the square—and that's what all these ' lookings-in ' mean, or I'm much mistaken. However, I'll say nothing concerning them to Scott—it would only hurt the poor lad more ; and he meant well, though he did rub Mr. Fulmer's fur up a bit the wrong way."

" Do you tell me your people are actually keeping on that thief ?" asked Frank one Sunday evening when he and Mr. Jeffley were returning from their usual afternoon's outing.

" Well, that's what they seem to be doing," confessed Jack, with mournful reluctance.

" I could not have believed it possible," commented Frank.

For a few yards Mr. Jeffley walked on in silence. He was a large man, and his thoughts moved slowly, like the pendulum of a big clock.

At last he spoke :

" If I saw a great hulking fellow thrashing his wife, I'd interfere ; but I'd be a fool, for they would both set on me. It is just the same thing meddling between master and man—the master does not thank you ; and the man, when he gets to know, which he always does somehow, hates you. Still, I suppose it's the right thing to speak. Even as this affair has turned out, I am not at heart sorry you did speak."

" I am then," retorted Frank, " sorry enough for both of us."

" Tut, tut !" said peaceful Jack Jeffley ; " what worse are you off than you were before ?"

He was careful not to say he felt somewhat worse off—that was Jack's way. He might not be extraordinarily clever—nay, as his wife averred, he might in some things have been considered stupid ; but in his faithfulness, his integrity, his loyalty, his consideration for others, and his desire to avoid all quarrels, he had on his own dull mental flint struck a diviner spark than mere talent.

Could he have so changed his nature as to speak hardly about Mr. Fulmer, and bitterly concerning a rogue and a cheat being preferred to himself, Frank had felt cruelly disappointed ; yet, inconsistently, no doubt, he could for the moment scarcely help wishing that even for his own sake Jack had " more fight."

Personally, it never once entered into the young man's mind that the information imparted—information procured at the cost of so much trouble—would or could benefit himself ; but he had hoped to benefit his friend. In imagination (on the way up to Hamilton Place) he heard Mr. Jeffley thanked and complimented ; after a time promoted to a higher post, which involved likewise an increase of salary, easier hours, and a better standing.

He was grateful to and jealous for honest, kindly Jack Jeffley, who could not have hurt a fly, or even Mr. Katzen. He had seen a way, as he thought, to help forward his friend,

who was not likely to push himself forward—
and behold! his dream and his visions re-
sulted in the snubbing and neglect of Virtue,
and the toleration, not to say triumph, of
Vice.

It was very hard, and, though in the main
amiable and generally meek and docile
enough, Frank undoubtedly did feel his
" angry passions rise " very often when he
encountered Mr. Gregson in the City and at
the West End, ay, even beside the counter of
that very bank where Rothsattel and Co. kept
their account, which young Scott knew, or at
all events shrewdly suspected, was only floated
on from day to day by clever " manipulation."

Clean-shaven, rosy-faced, easy-going, well-
dressed, plausible-mannered Mr. Gregson was
not at all the sort of person who looked likely
to be playing a double game. His bosom's
lord apparently sat lightly enough upon its
throne. No sword of Damocles seemed sus-
pended over that round sleek head. He was
as ready with his joke as in other days fire-
eaters were with their pistol. If he found
nothing to speak about but the weather, he

spoke of that with an oily laugh which somehow suggested the gurgling sound of rich wine in process of decanting. To the bank clerks, to the commissionaires, to the very police as he passed them, Mr. Gregson always found something cheery to say. " He was such a pleasant gentleman," everyone declared in chorus. Frank grew to hate him, and tried to make Mr. Jeffley hate him too ; but Jack declared that to be impossible. Mr. Gregson —though " inclined to be a bit stiffish and stand off" ever since one day, a long time ago, when Mr. Jeffley refused to deliver an order " unless it came to him through the regular course "—had done him no harm ; " and even if he had," finished Jack, " I would try to bear no malice."

Latterly, as his friend noticed, young Scott had become a little embittered. He had much to say about rich rogues, and men who by rights ought to be standing in the dock, driving about in carriages and pairs, about genius plodding along in bad boots, and the unequal battle brains must perforce wage when fighting against a banker's balance ;

but to all this Mrs. Jeffley's husband paid small heed.

" If it's any comfort to you, go ahead," he was wont to say. " Bless you, I've heard so much of this sort of thing, it seems quite natural. I thought you were holding your nose to the grindstone too patiently for it to last; we all make a noise and to-do at first, or at any rate it's best for us to try to kick over the traces before we've been long in harness—we work off our high spirits that way, and then settle down quietly enough. No doubt it appears hard lines, after having enjoyed our liberty, to feel the gall of the collar and the jerk of the bit, and that cursed bearing-rein, another man's will, constantly pulling us up, to say nothing of the constant lash, lash, of necessity ; but we get used to it all after a while. If we don't, it's the worse for us."

Jack's words were wise enough, and the younger man knew it. Nevertheless, he felt that his load was more than doubled by the spectacle of Mr. Gregson still keeping his appointment in Deedes' house, and at one and the same time selling Deedes' wine and the firm that paid his salary.

" There is not much encouragement in London for a man to be honest," he thought bitterly each time he encountered Mr. Gregson, so jovial, healthy, prosperous, and joyous.

Had he been able to look into Mr. Gregson's heart, however, his opinion would scarcely have remained the same. Even in that apparently stout and sunny residence Care had found a chamber quite to her mind. At first Mr. Gregson was scarcely aware of her contiguity, but after a short time he got to be as much afraid of that room hidden from the world as a child is of a dark closet.

Up to a certain point the plans of Messrs. Rothsattel and Co. had prospered exceedingly ; not a hitch occurred. The play went on with perfect smoothness—each actor did what he ought to have done, said what he ought to say, and retired at the right moment; the curtain rose, and the curtain fell, without misadventure ; the set scenes looked like reality, and the few necessary changes were effected under the very noses of those most interested in the matter, without a suspicion being aroused as to the *bonâ fides* of the performance.

Deedes had perfect confidence in their manager. They accepted his word as though it were Gospel. They allowed him to manipulate the customers. If he advised longer credit, then longer credit was given. If he said, " I think I should draw in a little here," a negligent or shaky debtor was soon made to feel Deedes, Tunstall, Fulmer and Co. existed in the flesh, and could sign letters far from agreeable.

This was a sort of thing which had gone on for years, and which might have gone on for many more, had Mr. Gregson's private expenditure continued to keep step with his salary ; but it did not.

By some means, he got into the " swing " of a very lavish and showy set of people. He began to supplement the dinners given for the benefit of his firm with dinners he imagined might advance the social position of his family. He had daughters growing up; he had a son at college; he had other sons at school. Either the wine-trade had grown worse—for in addition to his salary he received a commission—or Mr. Gregson's ideas had expanded. However that might be, the end of each year found his exchequer in a less satisfactory state than it had been at the beginning, and, like other great political and City financiers, Mr. Gregson found it necessary to frame a new budget.

He did not dream of retrenchment. The merchant or Chancellor who does that may certainly be honest, but he is generally regarded at best as a fool.

"When in doubt, play trumps," whispered Mr. Gregson, a devoted whist-player, to himself; and acting on this time-honoured piece of advice, he went on throwing out trumps till he had not a good card left in his hand.

In all branches of commerce a game is constantly being played in London and else-where, which immensely resembles the piecing of a child's puzzle. Given that the plan is put together as intended, all goes well. Given, on the other hand, that one part is either missing or misplaced, and everything turns out wrong.

Up to a certain point all goes well, perhaps too well. To-day's discount pays the acceptance due to-morrow ; the goods purchased on credit this week and sold at a percentage off for cash almost before delivery, suffice to pay rent or rates, or some other most pressing emergency.

Living from "hand to mouth" is actual affluence in comparison, because at least in that case what the hand fails to find the mouth has to make shift to do without ; but the claims of landlords, tax-gatherers, and Victoria by the grace of God, must be satisfied, let what back may go bare, let any number of stomachs stay empty.

Frequently during the course of that September, when Mr. Deedes still lay very ill and Mr. Tunstall remained in Switzerland, their trusty manager found himself considering as a not wholly remote contingency, the likelihood of receiving the most imperative invitation save one, which Victoria, etc., ever sends forth to her liege subjects.

Often matters grew very unpleasant indeed. Lawyers' letters, unless they contain tidings of a legacy, are rarely agreeable, and Mr. Gregson received more than he cared for of these missives.

For things had suddenly, and to his mind unaccountably, grown " difficult." Just as he had occasionally left Forest Hill bathed in morning sunshine, and found at New Cross a yellow, depressing, filthy fog patiently waiting for his train, so he seemed at once to plunge from a dry and pleasant land of safety into a sea of harass, among the shoals and rocks of which it almost baffled him to steer.

Aforetime, money in the City had been tight, far " tighter" than it was at that precise time, yet then he never experienced any trouble in getting enough and to spare.

Now, however, had national insolvency been imminent, he could scarce have met with greater trouble in procuring loans, advances, discount.

And what added yet another drop of bitter
to his cup, was that when he repaired with
his lack of success and heart full of bitterness to St. Dunstan's Hill, he generally
found Mr. Fulmer there representing the
firm.

As a member, and no contemptible member
of the firm, Mr. Fulmer certainly had a right
so to represent it, but Mr. Gregson did not
feel quite comfortable with that gentleman,
who had always held him a little at arm's
length. Mr. Deedes now . . . . Ah, Mr.
Gregson was wont to discourse largely over
the pleasure anyone might take in working
for such a "thorough old gentleman." Mr.
Tunstall, too, was "not at all a bad fellow"—
"fond of yachting, cricketing, rowing—anything, bless you, but the shop ; though, as for
that, Fulmer only cares for the result of the
half year's balance-sheet—never troubles his
head about how the business is made to pay,
so long as it *does* pay."

It was for this reason probably that Mr.
Fulmer's presence now seemed most disagreeable. Mr. Fulmer had not hitherto

been in the habit of putting in frequent appearances at the office ; and when he did, it was not " in any nasty, petty, meddling spirit, but merely to speak to Mr. Deedes, or exchange civilities with Mr. Tunstall." Now, however, of course matters were some- what different—Mr. Deedes being ill and Mr. Tunstall absent, no doubt he fancied he might be doing some good, though he only glanced over letters and read the *Times*. Mr. Gregson waxed merry as he described his principal's method of transacting business to some of those astute friends who " knew what was what," but in his heart he did not like this new departure.

" He's such a big fellow, he seems to absorb all the air in our small place," he remarked to Mr. Gustave Rothsattel.

Now Mr. Gregson, being by no means a small man himself, was scarcely justified in finding fault with Mr. Fulmer's still greater dimensions ; but the old sense of calm and freedom seemed disturbed by this partner's presence.

" Like going home for a quiet evening, by

gad! and finding some bore sitting in your favourite arm-chair," thought Mr. Gregson. Harassed and perplexed as he generally was about that time, the absolute repose of Mr. Fulmer's speech and manner chafed upon his already ruffled spirit.

"Just as though, because he is not bothered, no one else in the world could be troubled over anything."

Yes, it must have been trying. Distracted about money and debt and bills and bankers, he found it hard to reply with polished ease to Mr. Fulmer's condescending platitudes on the subject of the weather, and Mr. Deedes' health, and the political look-out.

Meanwhile, so far as the business of the firm went, Mr. Gregson was apparently having matters all his own way. If as cold as ever, Mr. Fulmer was at least as civil. He did not grumble, or complain, or interfere. He continued to glance at the letters, and to read his *Times*, while Mr. Gregson was doing very little for the firm, but financing largely for himself.

Still confident in his own position, Mr. Gregson indeed had not the faintest anticipation of a check from his principals, when one morning he received an answer which surprised him.

A bill of Rothsattels' had been maturing during those weeks when Mr. Fulmer was reading the *Times;* indeed, with that baleful haste to ripen which seems to be in the very constitution of bills, it was almost due. After it ran off, if it ever, that is to say, had the smallest intention of doing anything of the sort, Mr. Gregson knew another acceptance would be swiftly following in its footsteps.

For a moment he never doubted but that the matter could be "arranged" as usual.

Rothsattels wrote to Deedes and Co. a letter asking that the progress of the winged paper might be delayed by a "renewal;" they gave plausible reasons for their request, and Mr. Gregson followed suit by recommending that their prayer should be granted.

"Splendid business they are working up," he added; "they will be at the top of the tree in their own particular line before the winter is over; hard-working, sharp, honest fellows as any in London—safe as the Bank."

"Still I do not think we will renew," said Mr. Fulmer. The words were very few and very simple, yet they struck Mr. Gregson most unpleasantly.

"You do not know these people, sir," he remonstrated after a second's pause. "Mr. Deedes, if he were here, would say 'yes' at once."

"Perhaps he might," agreed Mr. Fulmer. "But then you see Mr. Deedes is not here, and I am."

Really Mr. Fulmer could be a very disagreeable person when he chose.

"Of course, sir—of course you are the best judge," returned Mr. Gregson. "Only I hope you will not be offended with me for pointing out that Rothsattels are very good customers, and——"

"If we lose them I shall acquit you of all responsibility," interrupted Mr. Fulmer.

"Thank you, sir, that is all I want; but we shan't lose them if any effort of mine can prevent their going elsewhere," and Mr.

Gregson walked out of the presence-chamber to make the best of a bad position.

"Has *he* been looking at the books?" he asked the cashier, who was an old man regular as clockwork, and precise in his habits as Charles Lamb's "good clerk."

"Yes," was the answer. Mr. Gregson had indicated the *he* meant by a backward movement of his right thumb over his left shoulder.

"Say anything?" further inquired the manager.

"Not to me," replied the cashier, as, with the calm of a clear conscience void of reproach, he ruled two red-ink lines and blotted them off.

Rothsattels' acceptance had still about ten days to run when the head of that firm in person called at Messrs. Deedes' offices and rejoiced Mr. Gregson's heart by giving a "splendid" order. Purposely, perhaps, he selected an hour for his visit when Mr. Fulmer was rarely in evidence; but he and Mr. Gregson had a comfortable chat in the outer office, where anyone who liked could hear what they were talking about, and where the cashier, still making entries in black ink and ruling red lines at the bottom of columns, was indirectly told what a large business Rothsattels' were doing—how that enterprising firm meant to take London by storm, and teach all who had gone before them the way to cater for the people.

"You shall see," said Mr. Rothsattel, in his ponderously deliberate German-English, with just the faintest pause between his words, merely sufficient to emphasize them. "You shall see."

As no one present except Mr. Gregson knew anything about that trifling request for renewal, the cashier, though so busy among his figures, may have been impressed by the statements thrown out in his hearing; but he did not repeat them to Mr. Fulmer, as perhaps Mr. Gregson half expected.

It would, indeed, as soon have entered into the mind of Messrs. Deedes' cashier to take a stroll up to Buckingham Palace, when the Queen chanced to be in residence, and suggest a friendly call on her Majesty, as to inaugurate a conversation with Mr. Fulmer.

To Mr. Deedes he had been known deferentially to remark that the prevalence of many rains, or the long continuance of drought, might prove disastrous to farmers— a class of whom he knew about as much as of the lost tribes ; but then Mr. Deedes was an old gentleman of a former day, and possessed of different ideas and manners from his partner. Mr. Deedes lived at Eltham, in what the cashier described as a baronial hall ; but, upon the other hand, Mr. Fulmer resided in a "palatial mansion" close to Hyde Park, in the very centre of fashion, amid the highest and noblest members of the aristocracy. His mother by right of birth was one of that charmed circle.

Her name often appeared in the *Court Journal,* and in the scarcely less select columns of the *Morning Post.* Of his own knowledge the cashier could not have sworn to this fact. But he owned for friend a most superior person, the widow of a major, who felt it incumbent upon her to do what she called, "keep up her acquaintance with the upper ten."

She did this, as many other people are wont to do, by following their movements from country to town, and from town to the Continent ; and she was wont to entertain her visitors with such remarks as :

" So the Duchess of Haut-ton has another dear little boy ;" or, " Of course you have heard that the Marquis of Honi-soit-qui-mal-y-pense is shortly to be married. He *is* so handsome !"

To the unregenerate this sort of conversation is generally more provocative of merriment than productive in the way of instruction, but it never wearied the little precise old man, who thought the dinners at Holland House could scarcely have been more brilliant than those delightful evenings at Denmark Hill when Mrs. " Major" Fitzwilliam " received."

She always made a point of being very gracious to the meek little cashier, keeping him near her, and saying in an audible aside :

" You did not tell me Lady Adela had left town ;" or, " Is it true her ladyship

means to winter at Nice?" or, "Has her
son gone with her to High Park?—all the
world knows what a favourite he is of the old
Earl, his grandfather."

After hearing Mr. Fulmer continually
spoken of in such a connection, was it likely
little Mr. Mott would venture to intrude
upon his principal's notice the vulgar details
of Mr. Rothsattel's eating-houses? — what
were "fittings" and chops, decorations and
jugged hare, cornices and Irish stew, to the
mind of a man who rode in the Park, and
could handle the ribbons of a spanking set
of four bays as well as any one of the crack
whips!

"Governor inside?" asked Mr. Gregson,
when, on the day that Mr. Rothsattel called,
he returned from some afternoon expedition
of his own.

Shocked by such familiarity, Mr. Mott
merely inclined his head in grave acquiescence,
but the action sufficed. Mr. Gregson walked
straight into the presence-chamber.

"Well, sir," he began, rubbing his hands
and smiling all over his face, "you will be

glad to hear Rothsattels have given us a capital order—capital."

"Oh," commented Mr. Fulmer. He never said he was glad, or sorry, or anything.

"They are thorough good fellows," proceeded Mr. Gregson. "I thought they would understand the position. They have taken no offence—none whatever."

"I did not imagine they would withdraw their custom," observed Mr. Fulmer; and then, as if the whole Rothsattel question were absolutely indifferent to him, resumed a letter he had been engaged in writing when interrupted to hear the good news.

Mr. Gregson opened his mouth as if to say something further, but seeing that Mr. Fulmer had apparently forgotten his presence, closed it again and retired.

When he shut the door he smiled, and sagely wagged his head. Perhaps he was mentally shaking hands with himself, while considering what a simple fleecy sheep Heaven had sent him to shear in the person of Lady Adela Fulmer's son.

It was no part of Mr. Mott's duty to take

official notice of Messrs. Rothsattels' capital
order till it had been executed. The routine
in Deedes' was for all orders to go through
what was called the usual course. After they
had done that, and were returned from Mr.
Jeffley's department as duly executed, then
the cashier worked his sweet will upon the
writing and figures, transferring both by the
aid of his fair copper-plate hand to two
immense tomes, labelled respectively, Journal
and Ledger.

Days passed, and the order appeared in
neither. Mr. Mott did not trouble himself
about the delay in Mr. Jeffley's department;
indeed, the whole matter had escaped his
recollection, when one morning Mr. Rothsattel appeared, this time during the absence
of the manager.

He wanted to see one of the principals—
for example, Mr. Deedes.

In default of Mr. Deedes he saw Mr.
Fulmer, to whom he explained he had called
to complain about the immense inconvenience
he was experiencing owing to the non-
delivery of a certain small order for wine he

had given to Messrs. Deedes' manager, Mr. Gregson.

"Yes," said Mr. Fulmer.

Mr. Rothsattel chose to take the word as a question, for he proceeded to enter upon still larger details, and to state at even greater length the loss and ruin such want of punctuality entailed upon establishments where "sharp" was the cry of one and all. "To a huge firm it may seem a small matter to keep our customers waiting," he finished, "but to us, who to live have to please the public, it is no fun."

"I can quite believe the delay has been no fun to you," said Mr. Fulmer.

"You are right; and you will see—you will give your orders—that we have the wine at once. I know accidents do occur, and a great house cannot always count upon the carefulness of all the little men it employs. It shall be now that we wait not any longer."

"Well, no, Mr. Rothsattel," answered Mr. Fulmer; "I can scarcely promise to deliver your order immediately: you and your customers will have to wait for some time longer still."

" How—how is that ?" asked the other. " Have you not what we require in stock ? What a pity—what a misfortune! If Mr. Gregson had only mentioned, we might have otherwise arranged."

" I have no doubt; but the delay has not arisen from any lack of the wine you require—we have plenty in our cellars hard by. The fact is—Mr. Rothsattel, do you want to know what the fact is ?"

" You may rest assured I do. For what else am I here ? What other reason could I have for leaving my business ?"

" That is not for me to surmise," answered Mr. Fulmer, modestly rejecting the posses- sion of such extraordinary powers of divi- nation as were suggested by Mr. Rothsattel's inquiry. " All I do certainly know is, that as you now owe us a large sum of money, we feel it better, for the present at all events, not to increase our risk."

" How ?"

" In other words, Mr. Rothsattel, for the

sake of a small profit we do not feel disposed
to run the chance of losing any more money
than we stand to lose at present."

"To lose! I fail to understand. I am
sorry to be stupid."

"I do not fancy you are so stupid as to
fail to comprehend that we decline to execute
your order."

"Why, what have I done—what has
Rothsattel and Co. done—for their orders to
be refused? If you want references—if you
have a desire for information——"

"If I had wanted anything, Mr. Rothsattel,
I should have asked you for it," interrupted
Mr. Fulmer. "I want nothing, however,
except to see your acceptances duly met."

"But I want something—and I will have
it!" exclaimed Mr. Gregson's good customer.
"I must know why you take an order, and
then refuse to honour it—why you keep me
waiting, waiting, expecting, and then say, 'I
never meant to send.'"

"Your own sense will no doubt answer
your own questions," said Mr. Fulmer, "even
better than I could."

"My own sense tells me a very good action might lie against you for breach of contract," retorted Mr. Rothsattel, in choked, blustering gutturals which he tried hard to render effectively defiant. "We shall see if people, no matter how big they are, and great they think themselves, are to ruin small men striving hard to make an honest living."

"We shall," agreed Mr. Fulmer calmly.

"I fail to imagine what your good partner will say to all this shuffling and double-dealing when the time comes that he is well enough to hear what has been going on while he lay so ill."

"*I* can imagine," said Mr. Fulmer, with unruffled composure.

For a moment there ensued a dead silence. Mr. Fulmer looked straight at Mr. Rothsattel, and Mr. Rothsattel strove to look indifferently at Mr. Fulmer.

"I suppose you have nothing more to say," at length suggested the latter.

"Do you mean you are not going to deliver that wine?" asked Mr. Rothsattel, in

a tragic crescendo. "Come, Mr. Fulmer—
confess you have been playing with us a small
practical joke."

"A joke—certainly not. Do you suppose
that respectable English merchants would
condescend to joke in matters of business?"

"I did not know. It is all so new to me.
Perhaps you have been suffering from the
spleen, the ennui. I was wrong to speak of
joking. Now I have been here and told you
all, you will give directions for our order to be
attended to?"

"No, Mr. Rothsattel, I will not."

"Then why not? Has there ever been
anything wrong with us? Have we not
always paid that we undertook to pay?"

"Well, really—as you put the question so
plainly—I am afraid I must answer 'No.'"

"No! Why no?—wherein have we failed
of our engagements?"

"I look back over your account—and I
find that against a large indebtedness you
have first and last paid the sum of seventy-
four pounds odd."

"That may be so—remark, I do not

accept your figures; but supposing you are right, have we failed to meet our engagements?"

" Yes, I think so—because it is we who have met them hitherto. With what I consider a culpable carelessness or foolish confidence—pray select whichever phrase you prefer—we have taken your valueless paper as though each bill were a bank-note. Now, Mr. Rothsattel, I intend there to be an end of this."

" An end of what—please explain ?"

" Your wish shall be gratified—an acceptance of yours is due next week. If it be not honoured, I shall at once take out a trading debtor's summons. As to what will follow after that, you had better consult some good solicitor—if you know one."

" Had you not first best consult your firm, Misterr Fulmer ?"

"For the time being I am the firm, Mr. Rothsattel—and for all time hereafter as regards you I am Deedes and Co. It did not suit my convenience to tell you sooner I knew your business was a mere bubble. Perhaps now

you will kindly leave me—*all business trans-
actions between us being ended.*"

"Der Henker hole Sie!" muttered Mr.
Rothsattel.

"I wouldn't invoke the hangman, were I
you," said Mr. Fulmer.

Mr. Rothsattel glared back at the wine
merchant, whom he had never even suspected
could be guilty of a knowledge of German.

"Talk of the devil, you know!" added that
gentleman cheerfully, as the customer took
his leave.

The days which that ominous bill had to
run seemed to melt into each other. They
fled—they flew. From morning till night,
Mr. Gregson spent himself trying to finance.
He wore out his boots and his strength all
for naught. No banker or discounter would
touch Rothsattels' paper. At last he tried a
document, which bore the legend, on its reverse side *bien entendu :*

"DEEDES, TUNSTALL, FULMER & Co.
"per S. Gregson."

"If you kindly leave this, Mr. Gregson, I

will consult my directors," said the manager to whom he submitted the document. " I shall be here at two o'clock."

But Mr. Gregson elected not to leave it. He could not, he said, think of putting such an indignity on his employers as having their good name submitted to any director in England.

" Just as you please, of course," said the manager, smiling ; and Mr. Gregson did not like his smile.

" I can manage this," said Mr. Rothsattel, when the difficulty was referred to him. So pressed for time were the confederates, that a hansom was hailed and the German drove off to see a friend who had an office near Bishopsgate Street.

" Where did you get this ?" asked the gentleman in question, looking curiously at the document. He was a compatriot of the Rothsattels', and ceremony did not obtain between them.

His visitor explained.

" And why did you get it ?"

Once again Mr. Rothsattel explained.

"Out of my way altogether," said the astute individual who had been regarded as the last plank between King Street and destruction. "I tell you the best thing you can do, though."

"Yes?" exclaimed Mr. Rothsattel eagerly.

"I suppose you keep up a very good fire for grilling at some of your places?"

"What has that to do with the subject?"

"Nothing, except take my advice, and put this into the hottest part of the fire."

"How?"

"Oh! you know. I wouldn't keep a paper of the sort if I were you. I wouldn't really. It's fishy—it's far too fishy;" and the speaker held out the document between his thumb and first finger, as if it really had a stale and unpleasant smell.

At length, but a few hours intervened before the dawning of that evil day which had once seemed so far off, so little to be dreaded.

Had pity been a sentiment in which Mr. Fulmer ever indulged, even he might have felt sorry for the desperate man who saw nothing now before him but ruin and disgrace.

Ere another night came, Rothsattels' acceptance would have been returned, and be in
the hands of the notary. Had he not already
exhausted every resource, there was still time
left in which to avert defeat ; but though he
lay awake in the darkness racking his brain,
he could think of no plan by which matters
could be staved over even for a week. Mechanically he dressed, caught his train, and
proceeded to St. Dunstan's Hill. Mr. Fulmer was there before him, and came out of
his office just as the manager had again put
on his hat with the intention of proceeding
to Rothsattels'.

When he saw Mr. Fulmer he took it off
once more.

"Come into my room for a moment," said
Mr. Fulmer, dispensing with any ceremonious
greeting.

"Shut the door," he added, when Mr.
Gregson obeyed ; then he went and took up
a position in front of the fire, while the
manager waited for what was to come next.

"It may be," began Mr. Fulmer, "that I
do not know so much about business as my

partners "—Mr. Gregson breathed again—
"but it seems to my inexperience that if a
firm have a manager, he ought to be sometimes visible. Now, you very rarely are,
Mr. Gregson."

"If I have been occasionally absent, sir,"
said the manager in a tone so low and shaken,
Mr. Fulmer could scarcely catch his words, "it
has been in the interests of my employers."

"On that subject I think the opinion of
your employers should have been consulted."

"If I have done wrong, sir, I have done
wrong with Mr. Deedes' approval."

"I imagine Mr. Deedes never contemplated
the duties of traveller and collector being
combined in one person, and that person our
manager. You do not seem very well, Mr.
Gregson. Perhaps you have been over-
working yourself and require a change."

Mr. Gregson placed his hand on the rail
of a chair to steady himself. He was white
to his lips.

"But for Mr. Deedes' illness, sir," he
managed to jerk out, "I should have asked
for leave ere this."

"You need not wait for Mr. Deedes' recovery before going away," interrupted Mr. Fulmer. "I dare say I can attend to the business—we do not seem very busy at present ; and as I intend for the future to take a very active part in the management, this will be a favourable time to look into many affairs which seem to require attention. I should therefore advise you to start at once. What do you say, Mr. Gregson ?"

"If you are certain you can spare me, sir—I——" but the end of the sentence died away, before the look in Mr. Fulmer's eyes, the curl of Mr. Fulmer's lip. "We can spare you," he said, "and if you take my advice you will go abroad." He added no further word, yet the manager understood that Mr. Fulmer knew everything — that for some reason the firm did not mean to prosecute him, and that he had better leave before Rothsattels' acceptance was dishonoured.

"Thank you, sir," he answered, "I will."

Passing from the inner to the outer office, he put on his hat for the last time, and without sign or salutation to anyone, left Deedes' for ever.

CHAPTER IV.

"I SUPPOSE he means, now he has begun, to make a clean sweep of us all," muttered Mr. Jeffley to himself, as he brought his face up dripping out of a great basin of water, into which he had plunged it in order to get in what he called "better trim" for an impending interview with Mr. Fulmer. "Well, I've done nothing wrong."

More than a month had come and gone since the day when Rothsattels' first bill was due. During that space of time many things had happened. The wine business in King Street was closed ; so were the various restaurants in which Mr. Rothsattel had proposed to give English publicans and sinners a lesson. Mr. Rothsattel was doing two things at a time—passing through the Bankruptcy Court, and, under a feigned name, opening a fresh establishment near the Minories. Mr. Gustave Rothsattel was open to an engagement as clerk. The other brother had accepted an offer to go to Cairo. In an unofficial way Mr. Jeffley came to know Mr. Gregson was taking a holiday, and that he would not return. Likewise unofficially he heard there had been something wrong in the accounts at St. Dunstan's Hill. To Mr. Mott no information was vouchsafed; but though little better than a machine, that gentleman could—to quote Jack—" spell and piece together a bit."

A number of debts were written off by Mr. Fulmer's orders as paid, though Mr. Mott knew such payments had never been made to the firm; and Jack shrewdly suspected many more might have been treated in like manner but for Frank Scott's word of timely warning.

" There had been no open unpleasantness,"

Jack gathered from Mr. Mott, between
Mr. Fulmer and Deedes' manager. On the
very morning of his departure they had met
"just as usual." "When Mr. Gregson caught
poor little Manley stealing the stamps, anyone might have thought heaven and earth
had crashed together," said the cashier plain-
tively, screwing up his face in disagreeable
memory of the vulgar noise. "It is just
three years ago ; you remember, Mr. Jeffley,
how a policeman was sent for, and the poor
child, for he was but a child, and a weakly
one, given in charge? I shall not forget his
mother's agony in a hurry—pretty woman,
too," added that sad rogue Mr. Mott, with a
simper, "young and a widow. Mr. Gregson
was out, and I showed her into Mr. Deedes'
office myself. For once I took so much upon
me. Straightway she fell on her knees before
Mr. Deedes. I would have retired, but he
called to me :

"'Heyday, Mott! what's all this to do?'
and then I waited.

"She cried and sobbed and wrung her
hands, and Mr. Deedes could say nothing

but 'My good soul—my poor soul—what is
the matter?' and he lifted her into his own
arm-chair" ("God bless him!" interpolated
Jack), "and made me pour her out a glass
of port, and so at last somehow she told
him.

"He was very angry—very angry indeed;
when Mr. Gregson came back I may say he
spoke very strongly about the matter. Mr.
Gregson said he only meant to frighten the
boy; but he was given to understand boys
were not again to be frightened in such
fashion, more especially the sons of pretty
and interesting widows. The lad and his
mother are now both in America, helped
there, I feel no doubt, by the excellent head
of our firm. And Mr. Gregson—he is—
Heaven only knows where; but I understand
there are men in possession at Forest Hill.
The house was mortgaged up to the hilt, and
Mrs. Gregson has gone back to her relations
—persons I should imagine in a humble
sphere of life."

It was the horrible silence, the utter
absence of a "row" about the whole affair,

which shocked and impressed Jack Jeffley.
There, "for a matter of three months," had
Mr. Gregson been coming and going, "sus-
pecting nothing," fearing no ill, and then in
one second the bolt fell, and he was launched
out on this world penniless, characterless,
friendless! Jack felt he did not like it at
all.   He pursued the parallel.

There had he been, "early and late"—but
that would "count for nothing"; doing his
best—but Mr. Fulmer might consider his
best very bad indeed.   He had put on no
new manners for the benefit of Lady Adela's
son—so that son might consider him "rough"
and "unbefitting."   All he knew for certain
was that he had stolen nothing—that in his
reign nothing had been stolen except a bottle
of sherry, for the robbery of which he cuffed
a lad's ears and kicked him out of the place,
making good the loss—as an accident—out
of his own pocket.

No; on the score of character he could
meet any number of enemies in the gate—
still he did not like Deedes' recent way of
getting on, and he disliked extremely that

somewhat peremptory note from Mr. Fulmer,
which said :

" MR. JEFFLEY,
  " Come round here at noon ; we wish
to see you."

Incontinently Jack stripped off his old coat,
threw aside his waistcoat, unbuttoned his collar,
threw back his shirt, and plunged his honest
head deep into a pail of water.   He came up
dripping, as has already been said, and as he
vigorously rubbed his face over with a towel
—scarcely less roughly than though he had
been a horse—he uttered that remark about
the probabilities of getting marching orders
which commences this chapter.

Poor Jack !—and he had not a halfpenny
saved.   Seeing his admirable wife " working
her fingers to the bone," he had felt bound
to cast the bulk of his salary into the common
lot.

For the remainder ? Well, he always dined
out, so as "not to trouble the missus."   He
found his own underlinen, and as the " missus"

had no time to mend, the cost even of that proved a considerable item; next, he had to pay his tailor—not much, perhaps, but still something. His Sunday visits cost a trifle beyond the expense of railway tickets, because Jack was no niggard, and so—as he said to Frank—"there you are."

Poor Jack Jeffley!

How many Jack Jeffleys, I wonder, are there in London, who, having done their day's work for thirty or forty years, take their day's wages, see it squandered by somebody else, and having spent a mere modicum on themselves, are annually buried by the parish?

A most sad and interesting inquiry—a statistic no political economist will ever obtain in this world.

" I never was one to shift and chop about," continued poor Jack, in mournful soliloquy, still towelling himself with unmerciful vigour, " and if I have to leave it will go hard with me. However, I shall soon know the worst —that's one comfort."

His idea that he would have to face some-

thing bad was not unnatural. He had long
anticipated what he called "changes" if, or
rather when, Mr. Deedes either died or
retired. Fresh blood would, he foresaw, be
introduced, and as a rule fresh blood is no
fonder of old servants than old servants are
of new-comers. Then he could not understand Mr. Fulmer, and with Jack to be unable to understand was to doubt. He felt
that even had he been wrong in going to
Hamilton Place, his good intentions should
have won him some consideration. He did
not like Mr. Fulmer's constant visits of inspection. He felt he had no right to object
to his employer entering his own vaults, and
yet he did object. Further, the quiet way
in which Mr. Gregson had been dealt with
increased his uneasiness. Jack could as
soon have lain in wait and stabbed a fellow-
creature against whom he had a grudge, as
talk civilly to a man meaning shortly to send
him to the right-about face; and Mr. Jeffley
unconsciously, but nevertheless very surely,
was convinced anything he could not do
must be wrong—in which respect perhaps he

resembled many other worthy and unworthy
people.

"He can do no more than discharge
me, anyhow," said Jack, slipping on his
out-of-door coat and taking a final glance at
himself in the triangular bit of broken mirror
which had served for dressing-glass to
the establishment ever since he went to
Deedes'.

In London, a wholesomer, honester-looking
face than Jack Jeffley's could not have been
met with, as, fresh from his cold "souse," he
walked towards Dunstan's Hill, smothering a
sigh the while he passed Fowkes' Buildings,
and wondered what his "little woman would
find to say once she heard he had got the
sack."

When he arrived at Deedes' there was no
one in the outer office. Even Mr. Mott's
stool stood empty. The whole place looked
as though some one lay dead in it. Its
aspect struck with a sense of emptiness on
Jack's warm heart. For a moment he felt as
if he had never been half fond enough of
Deedes' in the gracious and happy past.

As he waited, Mr. Fulmer appeared.

" Oh! it's you, is it ?" he said. " Go inside," and with a motion of his hand he indicated a wish that Mr. Jeffley should precede him.

Jack screwed up his courage, and pushing open the door of the private room, entered. The moment he did so, however, the fashion of his face changed. A great burst of sunshine seemed to stream across it. By the hearth, there sat in an easy-chair—the aspect of which was new to Jack—a familiar figure, Mr. Deedes—thin and pale indeed, but Mr. Deedes in the flesh, at least as much of it as illness had left.

" I am so glad, sir—I am *so* glad to see you here again !" cried Jack in the joy and fulness of his soul. " You can't think, sir, how glad I am! I hope you find yourself better, sir."

Mr. Deedes smiled. Ice itself must have thawed a little at the delight in Jack's tone, the fervour of Jack's manner.

" Thank you," he said, " yes ;" and he stretched out his thin hand, which Jack took,

and held as if it were some very rare and
fragile piece of china.

Mr. Fulmer regarded the scene with pity-
ing indulgence.   It was not business, still
certainly Mr. Deedes had been very ill, and
he was an old man, so he let the pair have
their little talk out before he said :

" We asked you to step round to-day, Mr.
Jeffley, because we want you to tell us if you
think any man under you would be qualified
to take your present place."

For a moment Jack looked at his employer
in blank and speechless astonishment.   He
had come prepared for dismissal, but this
request to indicate a suitable successor fairly
knocked him over.   Dimly there recurred to
him some memory of God having forbidden
a lamb to be seethed in its mother's milk, but
though he felt what the words meant, he
could not what he called " rightly phrase it "
at such short notice, and remained absolutely
mute and stricken.

It is, I fancy, our utter want of comprehension of the billows which may be tossing, and
the floods which are surging through a soul—

the struggles and mysteries whereof we possess no sort of knowledge—that makes us so
intolerant.

" If we understood—if we could *but* understand," is at some time or other the anguished
heart-cry of most of us, never pausing to reflect
we should then be as God !

After all, when we have thought as much as
we can—when we have reasoned as far as our
faculties will let us, when we have hewn down
trees which alone we thought intercepted our
view, and broken, crushed and bleeding, through
the thorns that barred our way—we come
eventually to as sudden a stop as Death.

To the strongest as to the weakest, at some
point in the mental journey, our Maker says :
" Thus far and no farther shalt thou come."

There is no mockery in this, for God does
not jest with His creatures ; only stern re-
pression in the Infinite inscrutable to our finite
curiosity.

We want to know all the ins and outs of the
great Hereafter—to have the Land of Promise
mapped out before us as though it were the
land of modern Egypt ; we fancy we can wrest

from science an idea of what we shall be when
our limbs are still in death, and our hearts cold
as winter's snow!   Pooh! and we fail even to
comprehend the hidden life of those we meet
day after day—eat with, talk to, think of,
love.

The highest to our vanity does not seem too
great a height to soar, and all the time our
blinded and stumbling senses cannot even
grasp the joys, sorrows, hopes, and fears of
the meanest creature with whom we chance to
be brought into contact.

"Well?" said Mr. Fulmer, breaking across
the silence.   He had not the faintest idea
why Mr. Jeffley's answer tarried in the
coming.   If he could have imagined the
long panorama of faithful service which
passed before Jack's mind as he hesitated—
the simple events, the stupid memories which,
crowding in, confused his brain—he would
only have felt amused.   "Well, is there anyone you can recommend us?"

With an instinctive feeling that it was right
to forget himself, that he must be loyal, come
what would, Jack took his courage in his hand,

and without looking at Mr. Deedes, who he thought ought not to be "brought into it," remarked :

"As you ask me, sir, I can but say what I believe. You have one man, and only one, fit to take charge——"

"And that man is——"

"Thomas Wilton."

"I suppose what you mean really to convey is, that after you there is only one competent man in our vaults."

"That is so, sir. I believe I am a fitter man than Wilton; but you see, you've as good as told me I'm of no use any more."

Mr. Fulmer looked at the speaker in amazement, and then a smile slowly approached his lips and hovered about them.

"He is laughing at me," thought poor Jack, "and I'd like to punch his head."

Already it will be perceived he was ceasing to regard Mr. Fulmer as a master, and the natural feelings of himself as a mere man were acquiring importance.

"Perhaps," interposed Mr. Deedes in his low cultured tone, to which his long illness had added a touch of gentle pathos, "we had better explain to Jeffley a little more clearly what we mean. He cannot exactly understand."

" I am afraid I do, sir. But——"

" No, you don't," retorted Mr. Fulmer. "You know nothing about what we have in our minds. And so you can confidently recommend Wilton for your own berth ?"

" Yes, sir, I can, though it's hard—remember, sir, I am making no complaint—it's your right, of course, to discharge and keep those you think fitting—still——"

" Pray proceed, Mr. Jeffley," entreated Mr. Fulmer, his smile increasing in amusement as Jack spoke. " Your original views interest me greatly."

" Sit down, Jeffley," suggested Mr. Deedes, with a movement of his thin white hand. " And do not misunderstand us. Mr. Fulmer is coming to the point presently."

"Yes, Jeffley, sit down," added Mr. Fulmer. " What! won't you ? Oh ! just as you like !" and he actually laughed.

Aforetime Jack desired to punch the head

of this partner in the firm he served, and now he felt he wanted to kick him—at last he was cordially at one with Frank Scott.

"If Mr. Deedes bids me sit, sir, I'll sit," he answered, "but if not, I think I'd just as lief take what I've got to take standing."

"It is all a matter of taste, therefore as you please. And now to business. You are of course aware, Mr. Jeffley, that Mr. Gregson has left us?"

"So I have heard, sir."

"And, in consequence of his departure, Mr. Deedes and I have decided to make some changes in the office."

"Yes, sir."

Jack's face was pale enough, and his lips white enough now. Well—it seemed like having a few hundred teeth out at one wrench; but it would soon be over, he again told himself.

"I may explain at once we are quite agreed as regards one point—we never intend any future manager to possess the power that was entrusted to Mr. Gregson."

" I shouldn't think you were wrong there, sir," answered Mr. Jeffley.

He could speak rationally still, he found, though his wits kept wandering off to the separation between himself and the old firm, and wondering why, even for the sake of " letting him down easy," Mr. Fulmer thought it worth while to mention the firm's future intentions at all.

" And, with Mr. Deedes' consent, it is better for me to tell you that at first he and I were not at one as regards making any change at our vaults."

" I thank Mr. Deedes, sir; it is what I should have expected from him. However faulty, I tried honestly—honestly, sir—to do my best; and Mr. Deedes is not the gentleman to despise anyone for doing no better than lay within his power."

Mr. Fulmer shot a swift glance at his partner, who met it with a doubtful smile and slightly anxious look in his mild, kind eyes.

" But I have persuaded him," went on Mr. Fulmer, rearing his head masterfully, as was

his habit when he met with even silent oppo-
sition, " that we can't do better than take
you out of the vaults and plant you here
as manager."

" As *what*, sir ?"

" Bless and save the man, is he deaf!" exclaimed Mr. Fulmer. " You are going to be
manager here at a smaller salary than Mr.
Gregson had, and affairs will be on a different
footing altogether. When all is said, however, the post means promotion, any way you
look at it. We will go into details presently;
meanwhile, I need only add, I hope we shall
get on as comfortably in the future as we
have in the past."

" Does he mean it, sir—really ?" asked
Jack, turning in his bewilderment to Mr.
Deedes.

" Mean it—of course I mean it," retorted
Mr. Fulmer ; " what do you mean ?"

" You are rather surprised, Jeffley, are you
not ?" said Mr. Deedes kindly. " Well, so
was I when Mr. Fulmer first broached the
matter. I did not see my way—I feared
that——"

" That I was too rough-and-ready, sir,"
finished Jack; " and I am."

" I don't care what the deuce you are, so
long as you are honest," struck in Mr. Fulmer.

" I am honest enough, if that is all;
but——"

" Never mind the buts now; we'll hear
plenty of them, no doubt, after a time. Anything you want to say to Mr. Deedes you
had better get over at once—as you see he is
not so strong as I hope he soon will be again
—and then come into the next office that
you may know just what you will have to do
and the amount we mean to give you for
doing it. What! have you not a word for
Mr. Deedes ?"

" I'm dazed, sir !" exclaimed Jack pathetic-
ally.

" Then the sooner you get undazed the
better."

" I understand him," interposed Mr.
Deedes ; " don't I, Jeffley ?"

" Yes, sir," murmured Jack faintly.

" That being settled, then, we may get to
business."

And Mr. Fulmer, opening the door, gave
the new manager a hint that all arrange-
ments with the firm being satisfactorily concluded, one of the partners was prepared to
enter into minutiæ with him.

" We are going to have in fresh blood," he
explained, when he had gone into the
question of work and pay. " Though I hope
we none of us intend to die immediately if we
can help it, still we feel we are not so young
as we should like to be. Mr. Deedes will
therefore bring a nephew into the office, and
I a cousin. Personally I have a great opinion
of youth—and, by-the-bye, that reminds me—
that stripling who accompanied you to my
house, is he still with the bill-broker in
Nicholas Lane ?"

" Yes, sir."

" Well—just ask him to call upon me some
day about twelve, will you ?"

" I will ask him," said Jack.

" You say that as if you did not think he
would come."

" I can't answer for his coming, sir."

"You tell him he may find it his interest to call here."

"I think that would be very likely to keep him away," said Jack mournfully.

"Very well, then—tell him he may *not* find it to his advantage."

"I will do my best, sir," which, according to promise, Jack did.

"It would not surprise me one bit if Mr. Fulmer handed you a matter of twenty or even twenty-five pounds," remarked Mr. Jeffley, after he had smoked for a few minutes over young Scott's first point-blank refusal.

"I don't want his twenty-five pounds."

"There was a time," said Jack meditatively, "when I thought a great deal of twenty-five pounds. I had to live very close, and look well after my sixpences, before I could save up enough even to buy my wife that gold chain she wears. Lord, though, was I not happy then!"

"If poverty makes a man happy, the argument is I had better not go to Dunstan's Hill," suggested Frank.

Nevertheless he went, determined to reject

the possible note indicated by Mr. Jeffley, and taking great comfort by the way out of the refusal he intended.

On his return, as he came past the church towards Tower Street looking grave and preoccupied, Mr. Jeffley met him.

" What's up ?" asked that gentleman anxiously. " Didn't he offer you anything worth having ?"

" Come with me," answered Frank, taking his friend by the arm and leading him into the peaceful retirement of St. Mary-at-Hill. " Now guess what your people have given me," he said, with flushed cheeks and excited manner.

" A tenner ?"

" No."

" A pony ?"

" No ; guess again."

" Can't," answered Mr. Jeffley, puzzled. " Give it up—perhaps nothing."

" Two hundred a year."

" You're mad, Scott—raving mad !"

"Oh no, I'm not—they are going to start a branch establishment for the sale of light wines, and it is settled that I shall take part charge as soon as I can find suitable premises."

"Anything more of the same sort ?" said Jack incredulously.

"Yes ; I am going this hour, this instant, to see whether those offices Katzen was always hankering after in Mr. Brisco's old house are still to let."

"Are you sure that is all ?" suggested his friend, with a fine irony.

"All at present;" and Frank Scott released Mr. Jeffley's arm, and strode down Love Lane.

CHAPTER V.

COMPATRIOTS.

ET a rose be as sweet and beautiful as it may, there is generally on its stem a thorn. Nothing more sweet and beautiful than New Andalusia seemed at first could well be imagined, yet Mr. Katzen all through the golden summer succeeding his appointment found the proud position of Consul for that favoured country was not without its drawbacks. To begin with, many persons were absolutely indifferent as to whether even a land so blessed in its soil, in its climate, etc., possessed a representative in England or whether it had none. This was very hard to bear, but Mr. Katzen found that the fact of being unable to impress and arouse envy in some individuals was harder still.

"For example," he considered, "take that great ox John Jeffley—he thinks no more of me than he did when I had not a notion where to turn for sixpence; his nod is just as familiar and his 'Well, Mr. Katzen, and how are things looking with you?' as unmeaning and lacking in cordiality as of yore. Then turn I to that Frank Scott, a youth of promise. I could have moulded and made a young man such as he. His usefulness to me would indeed have been great, whilst to him the benefit could not be calculated; and yet he looks as content as though he had not declined my offer, as if he were not still going and coming, fetching and carrying for the pleasure of employers who would show him the door supposing he summoned up courage to ask for an extra shilling a week."

Worse than these two examples Mr. Katzen considered the behaviour of Miss Weir, who mocked at the idea of her suitor making a fortune and derided the Baron von Katzen-stein suggestion to the suggestor's face. In this case what made him feel the thorn-pricks so acutely was that he did not happen to be making his fortune, and that the chance of obtaining a title by purchase or otherwise seemed to have retired into the remote future.

All these various stabs were trying, yet Mr. Katzen could have borne them had money not run very short. The way one looks at the state of one's own prospects is influenced, more than any of us would care to own, by whether our purse is full or empty. If full, how philosophically we can bear trouble, how bravely face misfortune! if empty—ah! my friends, there is so much implied in that "if," that you had better make up your minds never to let your purse get empty!

Should you do so, and see no means honest or otherwise of filling it, you will realize what Mr. Katzen felt when he found money had to be paid, and that there was no money to pay with.

He had gone too fast, not for the first time in his life; he had mentally sold his crop almost before the young leaves were above ground ; he had made sure in his own mind, and it is unwise to be too sure ; he had, as he himself truly said, played the fool ; in a word, he had quarrelled with his bread and butter, being positive he had but to wave his Consul's wand, and rich meats and rare fruits would appear at his bidding.   But they did not—he might apparently wave as much as he liked, and produce no result.   In the City summer is a bad season in which to quarrel with such portion of a loaf as Providence may send you. Experimentally Mr. Katzen proved the truth of this remark.

His bread had been often little and his butter scanty, still it was better than none. In his well-furnished offices, in his suit of fashionably made clothes (still unpaid for), notwithstanding the fact that he was Consul for New Andalusia, he found himself as utterly cornered as had been the case over and over again in Botolph Lane.   But there his responsibilities were few, and as a rule something "turned up" to help him over whatever difficulty might be pressing.   In Mitre Court, on the contrary, day succeeded to day, and week to week, and month to month, and matters grew steadily worse.

Mr. Katzen said nothing to anyone; but as out in the warm sunshine he walked the streets, hurrying from office to bank and from bank to other men's offices, he asked himself, "What the deuce am I to do?" till the question seemed by the mere force of iteration burnt in on his brain.

What was he to do? Clever and unscrupulous, fertile in expedients, plausible and false, though he might be, he had come at last to what seemed a dead wall in his career. And just when he had got a fresh start too, and all things looked so promising. Moreover, it was all his own fault—he had commenced crowing too soon, and received a moral brickbat for his pains. He could not get on any longer without money; there is nothing to be done without money—even a gold mine requires cash to work it.

"I wonder whether there are any gold mines in New Andalusia, or if that is all a lie of Bernberg's," he marvelled, not that it signified much to him then. Had New

Andalusia been paved with gold, it did not seem as though his position could be much improved.

" I wish I had not quarrelled with Bernberg, yet," he thought; but it was of no use wishing, the quarrel chanced to be a certainty which could not be undone.

"What is the matter with you?" asked Mrs. Jeffley one evening, when he seemed more downhearted than she had ever previously seen him.

" I have come to a brook," he answered— "not a very wide one, but still it is enough. I cannot jump it. That is all, but for me more than sufficient."

" I hardly understand," said Mrs. Jeffley, bewildered. " Are you in any trouble?"

" The worst of trouble; the old, old trouble —money."

"Why, I hoped you had done with all that."

" So another did—I myself. I was positive. It is bad to be positive."

" And do you want much?"

" Yes—a great good lot," he answered,

thinking with a sort of ungrateful contempt of the sovereigns and half-sovereigns and even of the five-pound notes which Mrs. Jeffley had lent, and which had sufficed in those humble days ere he attained to the dignity of his present uneasy position.

Mrs. Jeffley made no remark; she only hurried out of the room, Mr. Katzen watching her. "She goes," he thought, "to get her modest hoard, her two or three pounds—or perhaps seven or eight, shall we say, Karl?"

Karl was quite agreeable—deeming, and rightly, eight, though not likely to be of much use, would be better than none.

Presently Mrs. Jeffley returned. "Will that help you at all?" she asked, panting somewhat, for she had gone up two flights of stairs, and she was not thin.

Mr. Katzen unfolded the notes she placed in his hand. They were in number five. Mrs. Jeffley was smiling and almost crying.

"My dear soul!" he exclaimed. "What are these?"

"They are the rent," she answered. "I

am so glad I had not paid it; take them and welcome."

"And if the Rent should happen to walk up the court and knock at the door, what then ?"

"Why, it must knock another day, that is all."

"And if it says it won't come another day ?"

"It will though—it must; and even if it won't, I have money Captain Hassell asked me to take care of for him. I can borrow that."

"I do not like this," observed Mr. Katzen.

"But you will have to like it," answered Mrs. Jeffley gaily. "I feel honoured and grateful that you still let me be of a little bit of use."

"It is I who am grateful," said the Consul for New Andalusia, as he put the notes in his pocket-book. "Once again it is you who relieve me from a great difficulty. How am I to tell you what I feel ? I should think you were an angel, but that I prefer to regard you as the best and kindest of women."

" Do not flatter me !" she remarked.

" Did I ever so do ?" he asked. "*Could* I ?"

He was in earnest. Mrs. Jeffley had in truth done him what seemed an enormous favour. She had relieved him, as he fondly hoped, from the necessity of eating humble pie, than which no dish—not even the cold shoulder—is nastier. Out once again into the world—his world bounded by Lombard Street on the east, and Mitre Court on the west— passed Mr. Katzen. He crossed his typical brook—he pursued his way for a few weeks over a fairly level country, but then there came more brooks, as in the lives of all such men there must come—brooks wide and dangerous—brooks little but deep, without the vestige of a plank across them.

" There is no help for it," decided Mr. Katzen. He had judiciously sounded Mrs. Jeffley concerning that deposit left in her hands by Captain Hassell, and learned it was gone whence he could not reclaim one penny, namely, to the landlord.

" I thought it best to get the rent off my mind," explained Mrs. Jeffley, ignorant of the blow she was dealing ; "and if Captain Hassell should come back before you can pay me, I'll tell him I had occasion to use his money. Bless you, he won't care—make your mind easy about that."

Mr. Katzen could have made his mind more than easy had Captain Hassell's good bank-notes been transferred to his keeping. How-ever, as they could not, he deemed it worse than useless to fret over the matter.

" Either now or further on I must have made peace with that infernal Bernberg. Perhaps it is as well it should be now," he decided philosophically; and having so decided, he bent his steps in the direction of Alderman's Walk.

Mr. Bernberg was the gentleman who had procured for him the New Andalusian ap-pointment, having gained which, Mr. Katzen made the not uncommon mistake of thinking he might safely kick away the ladder by means of which he mounted.

When his countryman tapped at the door, Mr. Bernberg was " considering himself " in a cloud of tobacco smoke. He sat with his chair well tilted on its hind legs, with his feet raised on the back of another chair, a short briar pipe in his mouth, and a frown of dissatisfaction on his forehead. Mr. Bernberg was not unlike the first Napoleon either in figure or features, and any stranger looking at him might have imagined he was deciding the fate of nations. Like the first Napoleon, however, and for that matter, perhaps also the third, Mr. Bernberg was engaged solely in thinking about his own affairs.

" Ho, ho !" he said, in their common language, as Mr. Katzen put his head inside the door, and his accent was as beautifully guttural as the new Consul's own. " So it is you, at last !"

" First or last, it is I," answered Mr. Katzen.

" So I see ; well—come in. What are you standing there for ? What is your news ?"

" I have no news. I was passing, and thought I would look in."

" Very kind of you, I am sure. You don't happen to want anything, do you ?"

" No ; I have all I want, many thanks."

"Sit down, at any rate. Will you smoke? This is cavendish that never paid duty."

"Again, thanks, but I prefer a cigar;" and Mr. Katzen, suiting the action to the word, drew forth a well-filled case and lit up.

"Humph!" said Mr. Bernberg; "the Consul for New Andalusia gets his cigars cheap now, I suppose?"

"Very cheap indeed."

"And other necessaries?"

"Yes; and luxuries too."

"Including pocket-money, eh?"

"Yes; and more than pocket-money."

"Sufficient for the new Consul to keep a balance at his banker's?"

"Even enough to keep a balance which gladdeneth his banker's heart."

"Katzen," observed Mr. Bernberg dispassionately, and speaking from the right-hand corner of his mouth, the exigencies of his pipe compelling him to keep the other well closed, "you are the prince of liars."

"Much obliged; and then——"

"Why, then the same remark repeated, and then the same remark repeated over again. It is impossible to enlarge on such a statement. There can be no greater than greatest."

" Having conceded that point, once more I ask, what then ?"

" It is I who should put that question in another form. Why are you here—what do you want ? How does it chance you honour me with a visit—you who are basking in the sunshine of prosperity ?"

" I have said I was passing, and thought I would look in."

" So much attached to your old friend Victor as all that ?"

" Incredible as it may seem to your modesty, I felt as I came across the church-yard, where lies Shaughsware,* that my heart warmed to my old friend."

" The devil must be in your pockets, then."

* Principal Secretary to the Persian Ambassador. He was buried August 10th, 1626, in the lower churchyard of St. Botolph, Bishopsgate, the Ambassador, the junior Shaughsware, and the principal Persians attending the funeral. The rites and ceremonies were for the most part performed by the son, who, sitting cross-legged, alternately read and sang, with weeping and sighing. This continued morning and evening for the space of a

"You are wrong, my dear Victor. The devil is neither in my pocket nor my heart."

"Then I am honoured. By-the-bye, as you are on such excellent terms with your banker, could you get me a bill done, do you think?"

"Possibly—depends on the names and time it has to run. "Oh yes," he added, glancing at the document Mr. Bernberg held out for his inspection, " I am sure my man would put this through at once ;" and he would have taken the slip of paper but that his friend laughed and put it up again in his pocket-book.

"On reflection," said that gentleman, with another laugh, " I will keep this by me till it matures, or send it round to my own poor little one-horse money-changer. It is lucky for you that you have a big man for banker. I dare say he never troubles himself to look at the amount of your overdraft?"

month, and had not the rudeness of the rabble prevented, would have continued during the whole stay of the Persians in this country.

"No, he is very good about that," said Mr. Katzen, who knew if he had drawn a cheque for five shillings beyond the sum lying in his bank it would have come back to him with the ominous letters N. S. traced upon it. "And how is business?"

"Flat, confoundedly flat—flatter than ditch-water, however flat that may be."

"Things do seem very dull; but that is most likely owing to the time of year. Everybody who can lay claim to being any-body is out of town, except you and me."

"And we are here probably only because we can't afford to go away," was Mr. Bernberg's crushing answer. "My wife and girls are at Herne Bay—that is as much as I can manage this year. Lucky you, who have no wife and no girls to want to go anywhere. You must be rolling in wealth. I dare swear you have at least a dozen good irons in the fire con-nected with New Andalusia."

"No, not an iron. What is the use of trying to heat anything at a period when there are no fires?"

"I am not so sure about that. There is

plenty of money lying loose just now if one could but suggest a good investment."

" That is the rub," agreed Mr. Katzen.

" Had you only been wise enough to forward that venture I proposed early in the summer, we might have been rolling in riches."

Mr. Katzen shook his head.

" Well, unhappily, there is no use going back to that now. The directors have all been snapped up elsewhere. Ah, my God! what a chance was then thrown literally into the gutter!"

Mr. Katzen smoked on and said nothing.

" What are you thinking of doing now?" asked Mr. Bernberg. " I suppose you did not come round to-day merely to tell me the state of the exchange thermometer?"

" I don't know why I came round, except because it seemed a long time since I had seen you."

" What are you doing about the emigration scheme?"

" Nothing — people won't emigrate; at least, if they have to bear any part of the expense."

" I did not think there was so much sense
left in the world," remarked Mr. Bernberg.

" It is not sense, it is want of money."

" A judicious distinction, Karl."

" I am not sure that I should have accepted this precious post had I known all the
trouble it would involve, and realized how
difficult it might prove to get back any return."

" I am sorry to hear you say that."

" Yes, I feel I could have employed my
time to much greater advantage."

" You must bear in mind the day is still
young."

" That is true ; yet it should be giving some
promise of a blue sky."

" You are at last getting intelligible, Consul," laughed Mr. Bernberg. " Confess, are
there not a whole legion of little imps disporting themselves through the emptiness of
your pockets ?"

" No ; like the lady in the popular ballad, I
have still a very great fortune in silver and gold."

" Then what is the trouble ?"

" I want to see some source from which a

continuous supply of silver and gold is to be depended on."

" But, according to your old creed, sufficient for the day was the evil or the good thereof."

" Yes ; but then there seemed no use in looking beyond the day ; now, with so many chances within reach, it would be absolute madness to forget to-morrow must come, and on the top of that, probably, other morrows."

" My good Karl, if you have not the mildness of the dove, you have the craft of the serpent ; but to what are these mournful confessions tending ?"

" To the fact that I want something large and honest to operate with and on."

" Soh !"

The tone in which this was uttered cannot be described.

" I want something that will bear the scrutiny—something in its way stupendous, yet that need have no fear either of the sun by day or a policeman's lantern by night."

" Really, this grows touching. The

Consul for New Andalusia is developing a turn not merely for fancy, but for Realism!"

"It is one essential of my dream-project," pursued Mr. Katzen, warming to his work, "that there should be nothing shady about it."

"I see—I understand. Who was the man that said he would give twenty thousand pounds for a good character? Major Charteris, was it not?"

"I do not know, and I do not care. The man who would give twenty thousand pounds for anything except a freehold estate must be an abject fool."

"Softly, softly, you too impulsive countryman of mine own. The only reason this English ass, as you regard him, would have been willing to give so much for apparently so little, was that he believed he could make a hundred thousand out of it. Not such a fool as anybody might think—eh, my friend?"

Mr. Katzen shrugged his shoulders impatiently. Although, according to his own statement, his pockets were so well furnished, still there was not really an inch of his soul at that moment vacant for the consideration of any theme or person save the theme and person of Karl Katzen.

" I think not much of it," he said. " To a man with twenty thousand pounds in hard cash, what can character, bad or good, account ?"

" Much, I should say," answered Mr. Bernberg virtuously. " For myself, if I must choose, if I could not have both, I should prefer a good character to any sum of money."

" I do love listening to Victor when he gets on his platform !"

" I am not on any platform. I look back over my life and know to what I owe my success. How do you suppose I could have got along in this England where we are, if I had not been an honest man ?"

" That is a question I cannot answer. Put it the other way, and say, ' If you had been an honest man,' and I will try to guess," sneered Mr. Katzen.

Mr. Bernberg laid down his pipe, rose from his chair, and stood confronting the new

Consul, with his hands plunged deep in the pockets of his office coat.

"Do you say I ever cheated anyone ?" he asked. " Did I ever cheat you ?"

" Well, no—perhaps not."

" Certainly not; on the contrary, have I not done you good, much good, which you repay with insolence and ingratitude ? So long as you desired to be Consul for New Andalusia, who so meek, who so servile, as Karl Katzen ? Every day he came—ay, for three whole weeks—and it was only when arrived at the conclusion I had no power he ceased to climb my stairs. Then, after at last I got this good appointment for him, did he not offer lifelong service in return—ay, till he had pocketed my hard-earned money and was well floated off the rocks; but how quick came the difference ! ' Having served my turn you can go to the deuce, friend Victor, and my blessing go with you !'—that is what you said."

" When did I say that ?"

" Why, you have been saying it all summer in every action. When I wanted a little

favour, it was 'No, no, no;' when I asked
for my money, it was flung back in my face
as if you were lord of the Bank of England.
When I wanted a little information which
you could have got as easily as I can lift this
pipe, you found yourself unable even to put
a question to that Jeffley in whose house you
lodge."

" Upon my honour, I did put it, and got
snubbed for my pains. You might as well
try to pick a Bramah lock as Jack Jeffley when
the business of his employers is concerned."

" Then you should have picked his wife."

" He never tells her anything that passes in
the office."

" Bah !"

" Fact, I assure you; besides, I do not
believe he knows anything that passes in the
office. He is a fathead—a great blundering
John Bull."

" Is he ? Do you know, my Karl, I am
greatly afraid you are trying to humbug me
—me, Victor Bernberg."

" How humbug you ? What do you
mean ?"

" You are aware of that."

" In all truth—upon my sacred conscience —I am not."

Mr. Bernberg looked him over in surprise.

" For once, dear friend, do you know I feel disposed to believe you ?" he said. " I could barely have credited it. What a duffer, as the wise English express themselves, you must be !" and Mr. Bernberg laughed that hard, joyless laugh which we may imagine echoes through the gloomy shades of an unblessed hereafter.

" Will you have the kindness to disburden your mind of a secret which is evidently weighing heavily upon it ?"

" All in good time," answered Mr. Bernberg, still after his own fashion enjoying his own jest. " Let me see, it is scarcely six months since I made you what you called the most fortunate fellow alive. I dealt you a good hand—I would have helped you to play it; but, like a spoiled child, you pushed me away and cried, ' No, no, you go; I can do all myself.' "

" It is not the case ; but have it as you will."

"We were then in spring; here we are in autumn. You have spilled your cards—you have wasted your time. The talent I gave has been so long in the earth it is scarcely worth digging up. You have been a foolish virgin, my poor Karl; lamps filled over and over again have burnt to some purpose, while you sat waiting for oil to be brought to you. Pooh! pah! puff!—I thought you were clever and capable. I am disappointed in you—for your own sake, remember. As for me, I don't want your aid—I can do without you. Were you even to propose anything new I should feel it was bound to fail."

"You think me a sort of Jonah, in a word?"

"Well—yes, perhaps; he was a very foolish person, that Jonah. Self-opinionated and impatient—destitute of faith—disobedient, ungrateful—and foolish withal. Upon the whole, you are not unlike Jonah."

"Supposing that I am not—what then?"

"Why, nothing that I am aware of; only you may chance one day to find yourself cast overboard, where there is no friendly whale at hand into whose inside you may creep for safety."

" Ah, but you should remember how rejoiced Jonah was to get out of the inside of that friendly whale."

" Just like Jonah—he never even said 'thank you' for the shelter—to me, though it is of no consequence. Do you want any good furniture cheap ?"

" No—why do you ask ?"

" Only that if it had happened that you did, there is to be a sale at Forest Hill, at the once residence of a certain Samuel Gregson."

" Indeed, is that so? Then I can guess who pulled the wires."

" No, you cannot. I myself have no idea, unless it was your thick-headed John Bull— Jeffley."

" Absurd—you have not any knowledge of Jeffley."

" Nor has Karl Katzen, I fancy. It now happens that John Jeffley, Esquire, of Fowkes' Buildings—husband of your excellent landlady—is manager of Deedes', vice Samuel Gregson, cashiered."

"Impossible—quite!"

"Ask him, and you shall see. Other people in the world are clever besides you ; and now I must, much as I regret to end so pleasant a visit, ask you to go, as my business, like wind and tide, won't wait. Good-day, my dear friend—delighted to have seen you—so glad you need nothing—so pleased you have got beyond the want of a few pounds!"

" Good-day," returned Mr. Katzen ; "I will look in again the next time I am passing."

" Do ; and don't forget Jonah."

" No, I won't forget Jonah," said the new Consul, laughing with a bad grace the while he felt he could have shaken his dear friend Victor.

CHAPTER VI.

A GREAT CONCEPTION.

IN a very indifferent temper Mr. Katzen wended his way down Bishopsgate Street. There was no cause why he should have selected that route in preference to the back streets by which he had sought his dear friend Victor, but, upon the other hand, there existed equally no reason why he should have chosen any other. At that moment all roads seemed alike to him. New Andalusia, spite of its climate, its wealth of minerals, its unsurpassed situation, its advantages of soil, water, mountains, plains, forests and bays, peaceable population (mostly still unclothed—and so hungering and thirsting for the productions of British looms), appeared to him but as vile Dead Sea apples.

" Bah !" he muttered, with an expression of disgust, " I wish it had been at the devil before I ever had anything to do with it— and I wish Bernberg was at the devil too, with all my heart. He will be some day— would it were this day !"

It was a wretched afternoon; sky leaden, streets muddy, pavements greasy. No single item seemed wanting to complete Mr. Katzen's wretchedness. With empty pockets, in which a whole legion of demons were disporting themselves ; with a clerk to pay who must be paid (" I'll get rid of him, anyhow," thought the new Consul, in a sort of mental parenthesis) ; with creditors who had begun to ask for money ; with nothing on earth coming in except, at the rarest of intervals, a few uncertain fees—the look-out certainly could not be regarded as attractive. Nevertheless, Mr. Katzen had weathered many worse storms.

It was rather a dull sense of foreboding and sharp feeling of injustice having been dealt him by some one—fate or luck, perhaps, as he styled the vague fetish he acknowledged for deity—than the actual hopelessness of his position, which seemed so hard to fight.

Men who live from hand to mouth—men who are always feasting or fasting on the proceeds of their wits—are peculiarly susceptible to joyous or depressing influences. A turn of the scale makes them imagine henceforth they can play at football with the world—a straw causing the beam to fall the other way causes them the keenest anxiety. They have their unlucky dates and their fortunate days; they put faith in numbers, and find evil omens in coincidences; they believe certain places are propitious to their wishes, and that disaster meets them on other thresholds.

Destitute of religion, they are slaves to superstition; rash as children, they are as easily daunted. Secession or coldness on the part of those they even distrust and dislike, they instinctively regard as a sign of displeasure on the part of the one fickle power

they acknowledge.   It is hard for such men
to keep their heads erect and turn a brave
face to their fellows, but they do both—
perhaps because they know if once they took
to shambling along life's crowded thoroughfares they would soon be elbowed into the
gutter or trampled under foot.   The world
has grown so grey it does not want to have
its spirits depressed by the sight of misery.

As a rule, each man's trouble is enough for
himself, oftentimes more almost than he can
bear.   Life has come to be a great game of
brag and make-believe ; people lie nowadays
less on the chance of deceiving their neigh-
bours than in the forlorn hope of reviving
their own drooping courage.

Had he met anyone at that moment
willing to listen to his legends, Mr. Katzen
felt just in the frame of mind which enables a
person to perform the apparently impossible
feat of "lying through a deal board."   He
could have done it for the sport—to keep his
hand in, as a mere matter of good practice ;
but no acquaintance ran across his path.   It
was one of those dark days when nothing a

man wants comes within his compass. All this man could find to do was to elbow some lad out of his way, as though it seemed rather a pleasure to him to be asked, "Where he was a shovin' to," or "if he wanted his ugly mug made uglier."

After all, it is possibly a mistake to imagine adversity brings out our finest qualities—with some of us the cruel fire only causes whatever writing in our natures is darkest and worst to spring into prominence. That afternoon, had a twenty-pound note been lying snugly close to Mr. Katzen's heart, he might even have bestowed a halfpenny on the woman with sunken cheeks who for so many years swept (or perhaps did not sweep) the crossing from the corner of old Broad Street to the Bank of England, instead of negativing her suggestion of charity almost with a curse. Mr. Katzen was indeed in a very evil mood.

Coming down Bishopsgate Street he had debated within himself whether he should raise an internecine war by incontinently marching to Fowkes' Buildings and offering his best wishes to Mrs. Jeffley on the worldly advancement of her husband.

He would have liked to do this very much indeed, liked to forestall the news Mr. Jeffley had, he felt convinced, for some reason held back; but prudence proved stronger than the desire for mere pleasure.

"It would not do," he decided. "It would be good fun, but I might belike bring a whole old house about my ears—tumble, tumble, tumble—walls and chimneys and all —just at a time, too, when I have no other house to go to. She won't be best pleased when her stupid Jack tells her what Heaven has sent one day he shut his foolish eyes and opened his big mouth, but she'd be less pleased if I told her; besides, it may not be true—all Victor says is oftentimes not quite Gospel."

He had arrived at the determination, therefore, of keeping his information to himself ere he turned sharp out of Bishopsgate into Threadneedle Street.

"That is where the old Flower Pot stood," he thought, as he passed the spot

whence the "stage" conveyed Charles Lamb
and Mr. Minns to their respective destina-
tions. Mr. Katzen knew nothing about
Charles Lamb, and not much more concerning Charles Dickens, but his acquaintance
with London was sufficiently remote to
enable him to recollect how many omni-
buses, crowded inside and out, were wont to
start from that precise corner, and bear their
freight away to Dalston and Stoke-Newing-
ton, and Tottenham and Edmonton, as well
as to Hackney, and Shacklewell, and Homer-
ton, and the two Claptons.

He had seen men fight there for places,
just as men fight now for seats in the tram-
cars.

" Good Lord!" he thought, "I wonder
what has become of them all, and the negro
fellow who used to be continually standing
here. How London has changed, and seemingly not for the better for thee, dear
Karl."

As he passed the Baltic Coffee House he
paused for a moment and looked up; somehow, the greatness and grandeur of the bubble

once blown within those walls had never struck him so forcibly before.

"It was a big thing!" he repeated. "Ah! there were chances in those days!" and then his mind drifted off to the fortunes which were made during the time of Napoleon's wars.

Mr. Katzen must at that moment have felt himself sadly out of elbows as regarded his lucky coat, or he never could have arrived at such a ridiculous conclusion.

The giants of even fifty years ago were but pigmies in comparison with the plausible rogues of to-day. Then it required a whole system of elaborate machinery to pick some simpleton's pocket. Now, in the twinkling of an eye he is denuded of every rag he owns, and left stark naked, before he is aware anything special has happened to him.

Then, people bated their breath and held up their hands when the tidings of some grand swindle trickled down from the metropolis into unsophisticated country regions; now, it would be the merest affectation to express surprise at anything save honesty.

In this present year of grace, on hearing of some bigger piece of rascality than usual, we cry, " How clever !" Our grandfathers, who possibly were not much better than their descendants, on the contrary, said—" How wicked !" and really the words are not quite synonymous.

Parodying Carlyle's famous statement about the thirty millions of population, " mostly fools," it is scarce any exaggeration to state broadly that the inhabitants of all civilized countries are at this time made up of biters and bitten.

When a man tells you he has never been bitten, rest assured, supposing he is speaking the truth, that he is either a biter or never had anything worth biting.

No one recognised more fully the fact, that at the time of that South Sea Bubble, great, profitable, heart-enlivening swindles were but in their infancy, than Karl Katzen. He had seen a few nice things done. He had tried, not wholly unsuccessfully, to do a few nice things himself, only in those cases, hitherto, other men had reaped the harvest himself had helped to sow. That was what made him so sad and bitter. He could have cursed the prosperous men he met, whom he knew by intuition; only in the City it is not considered fitting to turn and anathematize aloud any passer-by whose appearance is repugnant to one's moral, physical, or æsthetic taste.

For which reason, possibly, he only blasphemed that lean-cheeked imposition of a crossing - sweeper under his breath; but, patience, friend Katzen, the day will soon be when you can curse whom you please at your own pleasure.

It is coming, it is coming fast. In your impatience the dawn seems long of breaking, but even in honest endeavour night must precede the sunrise.

So patience! Yours is not honest endeavour, though you would not object even to that if the gift were in you, and therefore the sunrise will be earlier. Already the germ of a great idea is about to spring into life.

You are unconscious of the fact, but the fact remains nevertheless. A lily bulb has no

knowledge of all the creamy beauty, all the
subtle languid sweetness lying folded within
its unlikely exterior, awaiting only the process
of time to stand tall and graceful in the golden
sunshine ; and though Mr. Katzen had not
much resembling a lily packed away about his
person, still in like manner he failed to understand that a chance encounter was about to
cause the conception of a project great yet
simple.

All Nature's grandest effects are produced
by means apparently absurdly simple ; and
who was Karl Katzen, as that gentleman
would himself have asked, that he should
attempt any superiority to Nature ?

It was the sight of a well-known financier,
who stood just at the corner of Princes
Street, discoursing to a friend familiarly as if
he were nobody—as though he had not started
more swindles and stripped the feathers off
more pigeons than any man in England ; as
if he had not provided in good time for a
rainy day, and so, when that day came, been
in a position to snap his fingers at judges,
creditors, Victoria herself, and the officers of

Victoria's sheriffs—which proved so inspiring to Mr. Katzen.

Why should he, the financier, that day be prosperous, successful, a very power in companies, admired and feared in the City, desired of all men, while Karl Katzen walked the stony-hearted pavements in boots payment for which he was being dunned for, and poor as Job after that fatal day when his " sons and his daughters were eating and drinking wine in their eldest brother's house"?

Not certainly because Karl Katzen was less of a rogue at heart ; scarcely, vanity whispered, because he was less clever ; assuredly not because he had ever felt inopportune qualms of conscience, or permitted consideration for others to influence any scheme which he had in hand.

" I'm down at heel enough, I allow," thought the impecunious Consul, " but hang it ! he must have been more down at one time. He wasn't born with a silver spoon in his mouth, lords were not his godfathers, or great ladies his nursing mothers ; he did not marry a fortune. At one time his name stank in men's nostrils. When he came to grief over that English opium venture what a hue-and-cry there was—all the little business curs in London thought he had sunk so low they could throw mud on his coat and he would never dare resent the insult! What a rush there was to the Bankruptcy Court to see dishonesty brought to book—my faith! I was among the fools, but I wouldn't have missed the sight for much.

"Abashed—why abashed? Never hold up his head again—pooh! the fellow held it higher than ever. Ruined—bah!" Mr. Katzen laughed almost aloud at the folly of those false prophets. "Why, he drove down to the Court in his carriage and pair, and he had a stephanotis in his button-hole, and he looked well and prosperous and hearty, and as if that moment returned from a long holiday out of town, which indeed was pretty nearly the case, and he said, 'I have nothing, nothing in the world. I have not sixpence of my own, everything belongs to my wife,' which came out to be true. In the prosperous time he had taken heed to his ways, and settled enough upon his good lady to keep the whole family, himself included, in necessaries, luxuries, and pocket money. Wise folks shook their heads and felt sure he could never show his face in the City again—he would be hooted out of it. Ah! ha! but they saw what they saw—before two years had passed, this wicked green bay-tree flourishing better than ever, financing foreign railways, getting concessions for Russian canals, netting fifty thousand pounds out of the Blue Valley Loan," at which point Mr. Katzen's reminiscences of a man so truly great and good came to a sudden stop.

"Gott in Himmel! Why should not New Andalusia too have a loan?" was the brilliant idea which brought him to a standstill. "She must want one badly, poor thing—she shall have it. She has cattle on a thousand hills, but no means of killing, or transporting, or selling them. All she wants is money to develop her resources; they shall be developed. Dear Karl, at last thou hast struck the right nail on the head! Ten thousand blessings on thy head, Deladroit.

How I love—how I respect—how I admire
thee!"

Scarce a second served for all this and
much more to pass through Mr. Katzen's
mind. He merely "paused on his step," and
it was done. Then he walked forward to his
office with a light heart and elastic tread.
He was a changed man. When he left the
Poultry behind he felt jaded, envious, discouraged; as he crossed King Street he
would not, to use an expression of Mr.
Jeffley's, have cared to call the Queen his
godmother.

At that moment empty pockets were
nothing, less than nothing, to the New
Andalusian Consul. The night had been
dark, and the dawn was not yet, but he knew
it must come.

For what amount should the loan be?
Not less than one million, anyhow, and for
many millions if well put on the market.
Out of those millions how much would stick
to the lean, lithe fingers of Karl Katzen?

Enough, at all events. He meant to take
care of that. It was his idea, his very own,

his brain-child. Karl did not intend his
offspring should bring no money home to the
paternal exchequer.

" The man who does not take care of
himself is a fool," he thought, "and I am
no fool."

It chanced to be New Andalusian mail
night, and he did not let the grass in
Cheapside grow long under his feet as he
hied to Mitre Court. By that post a letter
must go, apprising his Government that the
English people were wildly eager to lend
them money.

At that moment Mr. Katzen conjured up
a picture of John Bull, his breeches pockets
full of gold, which he was essaying vainly to
pour into the lap of fair, fertile, friendly New
Andalusia.

There was no time to lose. Somebody
else might behold the same picture.

Already a wiser rival might have discovered even greater loveliness in the dusky
beauty than himself. Deladroit, for example.
Deladroit, whom he had but just blessed, and
now most unreasonably felt half inclined to

curse! He, Katzen, would not miss this post, however. He looked at his watch. He had only just time to dash off a letter.

He was now at the corner of Milk Street, another half-minute saw him in Mitre Court. Hastily he ran up the stairs, taking two steps at a time, turned the handle of his outer office, and found it locked.

" Ho, ho," said Mr. Katzen to himself; "what's all this?" Then he drew out his own key, unlocked the door, flung it wide, and beheld total darkness.

" Soh !" he exclaimed aloud ; but, as he had no time to lose, he struck an etna, lit the gas, pulled out writing materials and wrote as a man might write for dear life.

" Soh !" he said again, in a weary yet exultant tone, pushing the letter from him ; after which he addressed an envelope, and folding his communication, thrust it into the cover, which he sealed with wax.

" Scene the first—act the first," he laughed, and taking up the letter, sped off to Saint Martin-le-Grand. He had not, though he arrived there panting, thirty seconds to spare; but that did not matter. The great letter was gone—the great project launched. Walking back to the office he considered matters more at his leisure, and found they were not likely to end badly for Karl Katzen.

With most earthly beakers of success, however, there is mixed some drop of bitter, and even as he in imagination sipped the nectar of good fortune New Andalusia promised to bring him, Mr. Katzen was un pleasantly conscious of a flavour of gall that somewhat spoiled the pleasure of his draught. Now he had posted his letter the want of money pushed itself once again to the front. It is all very well for a man to tell himself and other people he can get money, but it is not always easy to do so. Mr. Katzen knew this from experience. To go back no further than last Whitsuntide—but, bah! what was the use of going back at all? What he had to do now was to go forward, and consider how best to tide over the present difficulty.

With the air of one accustomed to such exercises, he took out all his worldly wealth, laid it on his blotting-pad, and counted over the few coins with leisurely consideration. The state of the finances was bad.

"Scarce enough to jingle together," reflected Mr. Katzen. "Matters could not well be worse, my Karl. But courage."

It needed some courage to face such a position, but it is true in London, as in all great towns, that no one can forecast what a day may bring forth. Even then help might be on its way towards this deserving man. Upon the other hand, it might not.

Debating this might and might not with himself, as he had debated the same question often and often before, Mr. Katzen drew forth his watch, detached it from the chain, and looked at it with eyes full of regret. Naturally, he did not like parting with his watch, even for a short period. A watch is a companion, a friend; in the eyes of the outer world a certain guarantee for solvency and respectability. No one could regard the entrusting of a watch—shall we so put the matter in order to avoid offence?—even to the temporary care of the mildest of Hebrews as quite the correct thing. Suppose anyone

asked him the time? He could not well say
he had broken the spring of his watch, or
smashed the glass, because in such a case
the jeweller employed would have lent him
another. Mr. Katzen sighed. After all, it
is not so easy as some persons imagine to be
absolutely respectable with only two half-
crowns and a threepenny piece in one's pocket.
Still, Mr. Katzen wished to be respectable.
Like Major Charteris, he was beginning to
understand that respectability may be worked
as capital.

Pensively he contemplated his diamond
ring, and fingered his studs, which Mr. Bernberg honestly believed to be paste.

"No, it is best the watch should go," he
decided. "Why—why have I been so
simple as to always wear these things? Ah,
wait but a little, we will all be wiser soon.
Anyhow, I can tide over till midday to-
morrow, and something meanwhile may turn
up."

Having settled which point, he again
slipped the ring of his watch on to the swivel
of that heavy brassy-looking chain he af-

fected, drew down his waistcoat, locked away his papers tidily, put out the gas, and passing through the outer office, laughed as he descended the stairs.

He was laughing to think that he should now be able to get rid of his clerk without a week's notice or a week's pay.

"And I will broach the subject of his coming to me to old Brisco. Ay, and good faith, I have ten, twenty minds to return to Botolph Lane. There I had mostly good fortune. Yes, I will sleep upon that notion."

Thinking much upon it even ere he slept, Mr. Katzen was making the best of his way to Fowkes' Buildings when he met Mr. Jeffley smoking his after-tea pipe. He liked doing this better walking along the streets than in his own especial den, in and out of which the cleverest woman in England was in the habit of rushing some score times per hour.

On this special evening things had been worse than usual, for one of the children named Wilhelmina, whom Jack, in "his stupid way," was wont to call Billy, was sickening with a feverish cold, and Mrs.

Jeffley consequently found it necessary to open and shut the parlour door at intervals of about a minute. Jack had wanted to go and sit with " the young one," but he was promptly told that "if he couldn't talk sense, he had best not talk at all."

" How do I know," asked Mrs. Jeffley, " what's going to be the matter with her? smallpox or diphtheria, likely as not ; and if it is, what is to become of the lodgers is beyond me to imagine."

" Won't it be better to have the doctor see her at once ?" asked Mr. Jeffley. " I'll fetch him in a minute," and he made a movement as if to do so.

" Just stay where you are," snapped his wife. " Do you suppose I haven't sent for him, while you were dawdling over your work ?"

" I never dawdle over my work," answered Jack, touched in his tenderest point.

" Well, stopping away then while you finished your work."

" I must stop till I finish my work," he remarked.

" There, I won't speak another word. Nobody can talk with a person taking them up short every minute."

" I don't want to take you up short," answered Mr. Jeffley. " Only tell me what you would like me to do, and I'll do it."

" There's no need for you to do anything. Mrs. Childs has been round three times for the doctor already. I am sure that poor woman must be ready to drop. Little as you think of her, I've but to say " go," and she'll run her feet off."

" Then, if Doctor Morris can't come, we must find somebody who can come," declared Jack, with unwonted decision.

" Yes, and see the child stretched a corpse before our eyes," suggested Mrs. Jeffley with a fine irony. " If you are going to smoke, I wish you would take your pipe and yourself out of the house. You can't help me by sitting here, and I don't desire the job of nursing two, I can assure you."

Jack took his pipe and himself into the street, as requested, and after paying a visit to the doctor, who was still absent, strolled

along Tower Street, thinking about many
matters, and wondering what could have
wrought such a change in the best little
woman on earth. Mentally, he had gone
back to the day, to the hour, to the place
where he first saw her. At that precise
moment Mr. Katzen stopped him.

"Well met, Mr. Jeffley," said he cheerily.
"Though late, accept my heartiest congratulations."

"On what?" asked Jack stupidly. He
had forgotten all about Mr. Gregson and
Mr. Fulmer, and awoke like one roused
from sleep to the sight of filthy pavements
and muddy streets. He had been dreaming,
with eyes wide open, of a glorious summer's
evening down at Gravesend, of a pretty girl
who was passing on to the boat in the company of some people he knew. Again he
could see the river, shining like molten gold,
flowing away to the sea—the vessel seemed
enchanted ground. When the girl spoke, to
his foolish fancy—as in the old fairy tales—
rubies and pearls dropped from her rosy lips.
That was the beginning of it, and here was

one part of the end : a miserable depressing evening in Tower Street, his wife mistress of a boarding-house for "all the tag-rag and bobtail" that chose to pay for accommodation, himself asked to get out of his own house, and Mr. Katzen congratulating him on his disillusion.

"Oh, come, Mr. Jeffley, you need not be so sly and secret with me," laughed the Consul.

"What are you talking about?" asked Jack. "What is the row?"

"There is no row, so far as I know ; very much the contrary, in my opinion. I did not hear till to-day you had been promoted to the post of general over Deedes' forces, vice Colonel Samuel Gregson, cashiered."

"How did your hear that?" questioned Mr. Jeffley, turning upon the German almost fiercely.

"A thousand pardons!" replied the other; "but I did not conceive you wanted it observed as a secret. Besides, it can't be, it is common property. Everyone who knows Deedes, and everybody that knew Gregson,

is aware you have stepped into a very good
thing ; but, of course, if you don't like me to
say so, that is a different matter."

"I forgot about Deedes," murmured Jack
meditatively.

"Yes, you were like a hen who lays an egg,
and, covering it over with a leaf or bit of straw,
says to herself, ' No one can ever find it.'
You meant to eat and relish your slice of luck
all alone, did you, Mr. Jeffley ? Well, eat
away ; I do not want to spoil your enjoyment
of it."

"You don't understand, Mr. Katzen," said
Mr. Jeffley. "I had no intention of offend-
ing you ; only the whole business scarcely
seems real to me yet."

" That is most likely," answered the Consul
amiably. " It is only bad luck—we feel there
can be no mistake about."

" At any rate, I was not prepared for such a
rise as this," agreed Mr. Jeffley a little awk-
wardly, "and I am greatly obliged to you for
your good wishes, and I did not mean, as I
told you before, any offence—only you took
me by surprise. How could I tell the

matter had got wind already? It is scarce a fortnight since it was first broached to me."

" It is true, anyhow, isn't it ?"

"Yes, it is quite true," confessed Jack, in a tone as if he were acknowledging a murder.

" That's right; and now let me tell you again I am delighted to hear it. When the news was imparted to me, I said to myself, ' I pant for the hour to arrive when I can take my friend by the hand, and speak to him the thoughts that are in my heart.' "

" I am sure I feel greatly obliged, Mr. Katzen," said Mr. Katzen's friend, who felt nothing of the sort.

" Obliged ! Am I a monster of ingratitude, that I should fail to rejoice when you are glad ?"

" I do not exactly know that I am glad," answered Jack.

" How ! What is this !" exclaimed Mr. Katzen. " I thought you never had the spleen ; that you in that were different from the rest of your countrymen ; that you never met trouble half-way, or looked into dark corners for it as women peep under their beds to seek for concealed burglars."

Mr. Jeffley made no answer, only walked on in sulky silence. To him, Mr. Katzen's thoughts on any subject at that moment mattered nothing, mattered less than nothing. Mr. Katzen could have laughed, did indeed laugh inwardly as he kept pace, after his fashion, with Jack's long loose stride. He knew precisely the subject which at that moment was exercising the mind of Messrs. Deedes' new manager ; and though he had no grudge against Jack, no hatred towards him, rather liked the man in fact, and certainly, so far as he was capable of respecting—which perhaps was not far—did respect many, very many points about Mrs. Jeffley's husband— possibly he was not quite so sorry as he ought to have been, to feel an inward conviction that Jack, big fellow though he was, could not, while he strode along Eastcheap, get rid of the pangs a coward experiences on the eve of battle, or,—to put the case less strongly—we all feel while waiting for our special dentist to operate without laughing gas or ether on that terrible wisdom tooth.

Jack's frame of mind was not happy, and Mr. Katzen knew it. He decided not to break the spell by a word. He had a notion who would tire first, and so in silence he, with his short legs, kept up with Jack's seven league boots, smoking a poor little cigarette against Jack's capacious briar.

It was Gracechurch Street, down which the Kennington and Brixton 'buses were dawdling, which brought them up. At that point it became necessary to cross, in order to go nowhere, or to turn back and retrace their steps to Fowkes' Buildings.

Mr. Jeffley stood, his feet planted on the kerbstone, looking across towards Lombard Street.

" Well," he said, " what shall we do ?"

" If the question is addressed to me, and I may take the liberty of replying to it," answered Mr. Katzen, " I should suggest returning to the warmest and pleasantest house in London by the shortest route. What do you say ?"

"All right," agreed Mr. Jeffley with an expression of countenance which signified he felt everything was wrong.

Mentally Mr. Katzen shook hands with himself, but he spoke no word.

He had determined Jack should take the initiative, which at length almost in desperation Jack did.

"Have you offered your congratulations to my wife also, Mr. Katzen?" he asked, taking the pipe from his mouth, and making a feint of examining it closely.

"I!" repeated Mr. Katzen. "I have not seen Mrs. Jeffley since I heard of your good fortune, and, if I had, I should not have thought of congratulating her."

"Why not?"

"Because I imagined, for some good reason, you had not yet told her the great news."

"As a matter of fact, I have not yet told her," said Jack; "but how you came to the knowledge I had not, baffles me."

"Oh, that is quite simple," laughed Mr. Katzen. "If you had, she would have told me — for certain she would have told me."

" Yes, I suppose she would," agreed Mr. Jeffley bitterly.

" And I would not forestall your communication for the world," proceeded Mr. Katzen; "my principle is never to interfere between man and wife—with the joy or the bitterness of matrimonial life, not for much money would I meddle."

Few things could have pleased Mr. Jeffley more at that moment than to kick the New Andalusian Consul across the street. He could have done it easily, but he refrained.

He made no comment even on the wisdom and generosity of Mr. Katzen's statement.

" The little cur, he is always interfering and meddling," thought poor Jack—which, as has been said before, was a mistake.

" Do you know, Mr. Jeffley,' said the Consul, "that sometimes it seems to me you think I am not your friend."

" That's a queer sort of notion, too," answered Mr. Jeffley uneasily. (" Hang the

fellow, he can tell even what is passing through
my mind," he reflected.)

"It is a queer notion," agreed Mr. Katzen,
"very queer—for who should be your friend
if not a man who is bound to you by ties of
gratitude and long acquaintance? I do not
know why you doubt me—unless it is because
it was not my good fortune to be born an
Englishman—but people can't help where
they are born, and I fancy it does not make
much difference in reality. If you had first
seen the light in Germany, you would have
been just as honest, as straightforward,
as unselfish, and as kind as you are
now."

Mr. Jeffley did not believe that he would
have been anything of the sort, but he could
scarcely say so to a German; further, the
implied flattery was pleasant. Though he
made a wry face the while, he swallowed it,
not wholly reluctantly.

"Anyhow, whether you think me your
friend or not," went on Mr. Katzen, "I am
going to take the liberty of one, and give you
a small piece of advice. Tell your wife of

your excellent fortune before anybody else has the chance."

" I was only waiting till I saw how things went on," explained Jack Jeffley weakly.

" Don't wait, then—don't wait an hour, a minute. You can't go on hiding such a light under a bushel ; and if I understand anything of your dear wife's nature—and I flatter myself I do understand much—it would hurt her to hear so excellent a piece of good news from strangers, instead of from one who is her all-in-all."

Once again the desire to do Mr. Katzen some bodily injury was strong in Jack's heart, but he could not deny the wisdom of his friend's advice.

" It's truth, if the devil spoke it," he muttered to himself. " Supposing Mrs. J. did hear of this from anybody else, there would be the deuce and all to pay."

" Good news is not long of telling," he answered, with a poor assumption of cheerfulness, " and I will get mine off my mind to-night."

" Do, whenever you go in, and then I can

felicitate her with an easy mind. It does not seem but the other evening when I met you and Scott in this very street, and we all went in together, and I asked you to rejoice with me. Now, again, we can all rejoice together."

"Thank you, it is very kind of you," said Mr. Jeffley, in a tone almost of relief. "It is a great rise for a man like me, Mr. Katzen, I am not ashamed to confess—a wonderful rise, so wonderful that I sometimes feel it is almost too big for me ; but I dare say I shall get used to my promotion in time. Talking of last Whit Monday, you took a bit of supper with us then. Will you have a morsel of something with us to-night ? The missus is rather upset about Billy—the child is ailing—and I was just wondering, when I met you, what I could buy that my poor wife would fancy. She's regularly upset, and you know when there's illness about she never thinks of herself."

"That means madam is in a fine temper," thought Mr. Katzen, "and this poor wretch has been having a taste of its quality."

"Don't you know what to get for the kind soul?" he said aloud. "I can tell you —oysters. Let us order some; or, if you like to go on and get your little talk over, I will see they are sent round."

"There is no such hurry as all that comes to," answered Jack, deferring the evil moment; "we'll walk together. Oysters—yes, a capital thought of yours, Mr. Katzen. I am really very much obliged to you."

But the food has still to be invented which could have propitiated Mrs. Jeffley that night. She was very angry about Jack's offering; it was just like him to go spending a lot of money when she had ordered a good supper for him—a nice veal pie cold, and hot sausages and mashed potatoes—and now it was all wasted.

"It's no use my trying to save, and manage, and make things comfortable on little, when I've a husband who thinks nothing of spending as much on a meal as would keep us all for a day. It is nonsense saying you bought oysters for me, because you know I could not touch one of them."

"Oh! yes, you will, Mrs. Jeffley," interposed Mr. Katzen ; "you will come and sit down with us comfortably, and make our pleasure complete."

" That is so very likely," retorted Mrs. Jeffley, with scathing irony, " and the doctor just gone after leaving orders Mina must have linseed poultices, and her feet in mustard and water, and not a soul to see to anything but myself. I might as well be a galley slave."

" Don't say that, Maria," remonstrated Mr. Jeffley, " and don't be putting yourself out so much about Billy, more particularly now you know there's nothing worse the matter with her than a bad cold. Do sit down like a good creature, and listen to what I have got to tell you."

" I dare say, and leave the child tossing about all by herself, with her face as red as fire."

" I will sit with her, Mrs. Jeffley," said Frank Scott, who earnestly desired to get out of the way while Mr. Jeffley imparted his news.

" Well, thank you if you will — she's

always quiet with you. I'll be up in a few minutes, when I have heard this wonderful story. No, I'll not sit down, Mr. Katzen—I can hear standing, and am not likely to be kept so long. Now, Mr. Jeffley, what is it?"

" I have got a rise at the office——"

"Oh, indeed! it has been long enough coming. I hope it is something worth talking about."

" Very well worth talking about—they have made me manager."

" And what have they made Mr. Gregson?"

" Mr. Gregson has left."

Mrs. Jeffley opened the sideboard drawer and shut it; then she looked into the cellaret, as though in search of something; then she went on her knees and examined the shelves with great attention.

"Won't you say you are glad, dear?" asked Mr. Jeffley, in a tone which touched even Mr. Katzen.

" Glad!" he interposed. " Of course she is glad—too glad to speak; is it not so, Mrs. Jeffley?"

"Oh, I don't know," answered that lady, rising from her inspection of the sideboard. "I don't think much of these sort of things. When people once begin chopping and changing, there is no telling where they may end. Mr. Gregson has gone now; likely as not Mr. Jeffley may go next."

Having uttered which genial remark, Mrs. Jeffley marched out of the room, leaving the door wide open behind her.

Mr. Katzen did not look at Jack, neither did Jack look at Mr. Katzen; the pair swallowed their oysters almost in silence—they had both been snubbed. Nevertheless, they did ample justice to their viands. Ever since the new dignity was thrust upon him, Jack had been "off his feed;" now his wife knew, he made up for lost time. Mr. Katzen could not remember ever having seen him compass such a meal, and mentally congratulated himself upon the excellent advice he had given Mr. Jeffley.

"She's as angry as she can be," he thought, "but the worst is over."

He did not guess that Mrs. Jeffley was

keeping a very nasty rap over the knuckles in reserve for him as he went upstairs to bed.

"Captain Hassell is back," she said, stopping him at the top of the first flight.

"And how is the worthy Captain?" asked Mr. Katzen.

"He seems well enough. He wants his money, though."

"Naturally."

"He can have it, I suppose?"

"Without a doubt."

"Now, that is a nice sort of pillow to give a man to lay an aching head on," considered Mr. Katzen, as he betook himself to rest; "but wait a little, my very dear madam—you wait a while."

CHAPTER VII.

IN THE OLD HOUSE.

AFTER all, Mr. Katzen did not pass a sleepless night, even on that uneasy pillow.

As he truly said, he knew Mrs. Jeffley pretty well, and understood she had merely dealt him this back-handed blow because she was angry with her husband.

"And if he does not cut her claws soon they will grow so long as to become dangerous," decided Mr. Katzen. "Bah! she is as great a baby as a child that thumps the table because he has knocked his head. Anyhow, my friend, you forget one thing—it is you who will have to settle with the Captain, not I; and these matrimonial amenities of yours grow a little too frequent and demonstrative. Years do not appear to improve the temper any more than the complexion. But why waste time in considering such matters? Good-night — good-night, Maria; may the dawn find you in a happier mood!"

Whether the dawn did so or not, Mr. Katzen never knew, for he saw nothing of his landlady ere proceeding to Mitre Court. Jack had gone to St. Dunstan's Hill early, perhaps to get out of the way of the possible tail-end of last night's shower; but Mrs. Childs—her face in its early morning state of astonishing cleanliness, and her person girt round with an apron white as Sophia could brush and boil and blue it—was well in evidence. From her he ascertained that the " dear child had never closed its eyes till nigh upon five o'clock, and that poor missus was so worn out she—Mrs. Childs— had persuaded her not to get up, but just try to swallow a cup of hot tea and rest herself a bit, which, goodness knows," finished the worthy woman, "is a thing she doesn't often do."

"There are not many like her," remarked Mr. Katzen, with more truth than might appear on the surface.

"There's nobody like her, sir," amended Mrs. Childs—to which the new Consul replied, in gutturals deep with feeling :

"Indeed, you are quite right."

He had three things in his mind that day, however, which perhaps excused less consideration of the best of women's virtues and anxieties than Mrs. Childs insisted were her meed. He wanted to trap his clerk, and he wished also to see Mr. Brisco. Further, he determined to lose no time in shoving the New Andalusian loan from shore. The first idea which occurred to him when he heard the news of Captain Hassell's advent, was that it would be absolute folly for him to delay proceedings till he heard from headquarters. He could do a great deal at once, and he meant to do it ; but before he did anything he must get some money.

Altogether, Mr. Katzen had enough to employ his brain without thinking much about Mrs. Jeffley. While that lady assumed the character of guardian angel, it had been all very well to turn to her in trouble and appeal to her as a friend, but things were changed a little. Of late Mrs. Jeffley seemed more captious than formerly.

" A woman should never show much of her teeth, save in a smile," was one of Mr. Katzen's axioms, and on this especial morning he added another : " If she goes on losing her temper she will lose her lodgers ; and then, what a life she will lead her Jack !"

The Consul arrived at his office before that slothful clerk, and was rewarded, almost before he had opened the morning letters, by some fees, which proved most acceptable.

He had the pleasure also of hearing they might have been in his pocket on the previous afternoon, had anyone chanced to be in the way to receive them. Rare, if not rich, were the few that came in his way hitherto, and Mr. Katzen felt, not unnaturally, inclined to regard this visitor as a " lucky foot."

The Consul was most affable, and talked long and exhaustively on the subject of New Andalusia. He wanted to get his hand in, to

warm to his work ; and finding the Captain—
who required papers—knew a great deal
more about the land of promise than himself,
obtained an amount of information concerning
harbours, tides, produce, rivers, and capabilities, which he made very good use of later on.

More than once during the conference it
occurred to Mr. Katzen that since Whitsuntide he had been somewhat neglectful of fair
Andalusia—that, running morning, noon, and
night, after a shadow he never could catch, he
had missed an actual substance close at hand.

What is a man to do, though, when he has
no money, and needs it ?

Like Esau, Mr. Katzen would often have
sold any number of birthrights for that
modern equivalent of a mess of pottage, a
five-pound note. Who, knowing what London is to a man needing money, and lacking
it, could greatly blame him ? Yet, sitting
listening to the voice of this unconscious
charmer, Mr. Katzen greatly blamed himself.

Here was a preacher who, all unknown to
himself, wrought a great, if not very efficacious,
change in a man by the power of one single

sermon. Never, for ever hereafter, Mr.
Katzen resolved, would he pay a debt to
discharge which he had to neglect his business
or to stint or embarrass himself. It was abject
folly. No; he could see how utterly wrong
his half-hearted policy of right had been.
Paying debts could by no process of human
reasoning be considered to have done him
any good; quite the contrary, it had done
him harm, stultified him. The more a man
pays, the more he is expected to pay. If he
is eventually to be hung, it may be just as
well for a cow as a calf; the cow's death
won't make the rope feel a bit heavier round
his neck than the calf's. When his visitor
took his departure Mr. Katzen breathed a
sigh of relief, just as one who has long been
groping through darkness gasps at the sight
of light.

Heretofore the person did not live who
could accuse Mr. Katzen—impartially—of
being honest. Yet hitherto he had dis-
charged a few unnecessary debts. For the
future he meant to reform his ways, and
consider no one but himself. After all, to

whom ought he to be kinder? Who would
consider Karl Katzen if he failed to do so?

With those fees in his pocket, which he
intended to spend entirely for the benefit of
Karl Katzen, that gentleman, after partaking
of a modest luncheon, betook himself to
Botolph Lane.

He concluded Mr. Brisco was not at home,
but he found Miss Weir in her accustomed
place, stitching away as usual. A person
much less astute than the Consul for New
Andalusia must have seen that the girl looked
weary and worn, and that her eyes bore traces
either of sad thought or of recent sorrowful
tears.

"And after this long time, how is my
Abigail?" asked Mr. Katzen, holding Miss
Weir's hand in his as he put the question.

"Haven't a notion," replied Miss Weir.
"Who is she?"

"Why, you, my dear darling—who else?"

"But, you see, I am not your Abigail."

"You will be though—some day."

"Were I you, I think I would not forecast
the future. Remember, there's 'many a slip

'twixt the cup and the lip,' and I have still a voice in the matter."

" So you have, and we shall hear it when you say, ' I will take this man for better, for worse.' "

" What man ?"

" Why, me—Karl Katzen."

" No, Karl Katzen ; I think not."

" But I am sure so."

" And I am sure—not."

" Well, as I said before, we shall see."

" Yes, as *I* said before, we shall see."

" Let me think, my lofe ; it is over six months since we agreed to defer the second reading of a certain bill."

" And now I propose that we take it as read," returned the girl. " Let it lie on the table."

Mr. Katzen laughed. " I do not know much about your ways of proceeding in your House of Commons, but I fancy you have somehow got mixed. Let us, however, as you propose, let it lie for the present."

" For ever," interpolated Abigail.

" For the present," repeated Mr. Katzen

firmly; "till I have finished making my big fortune, and can claim my bride."

"You have not made your big fortune yet, then?" asked Abigail.

"No, not yet; but it won't be long first, and then you will come to me. Oh yes; you will come to me."

"Time enough to talk of that when you have bought your title and your castle on the Rhine," replied the girl.

"Ah, you say so because you do not believe I shall ever get either; but you mistake—you make a great mistake, my lofe."

Apparently Abigail did not consider this statement required any comment, for she only gave a little laugh and went on with her work. Mr. Katzen watched her for a minute or two. He felt it pleasant thus to watch her: so round, so trim, so compact, so complete a young maiden is not often to be met. Her cheap dress fitted her to perfection; her cuffs and collar were miracles of whiteness; she wore a coquettish apron, in one of the pockets of which she carried her scissors and a reel of cotton ; in and out glanced her busy needle ; the room was warm and comfortable. Spite of the poor furniture and the dull light of a winter's day, which held no sign or promise of sunshine, there was a wonderful depth of peace and sense of home pervading the atmosphere. Mr. Katzen felt he could have sat on for ever, regarding that young face, generally so piquant, now so grave and quiet ; listening to the slow tick-tick of the old eight-day clock, and the rustling of the fire as the hot, glowing embers burnt away.

Something was missing, however ; something had changed. For a time he felt only vaguely conscious of a want, then he began dimly to wonder what the place lacked.

Suddenly it occurred to him.

" Where is the canary, Abigail ?" he asked.

" Dead."

" Is that what you have been crying about ?"

She nodded.

" Don't cry any more, then ; I will get you another."

" Won't have it, thank you," she answered.

" Why not ?"

" It would not be the same, and I should hate to hear it."

" Nonsense !"

" No nonsense at all ; sense, fact, truth."

" What pet shall I get you, then ?" asked Mr. Katzen.

" None, if you please ;" and there ensued another silence.

" Where did you buy that canary, Abigail?" inquired Mr. Katzen at last.

" Nowhere ; I did not buy it."

" How did you come by it, then ?"

" It was given to me."

" Who gave it to you."

" A friend, if you must know."

" Of course I must know. That young man round the corner ?"

" Yes, that young man round the corner."

" Which corner ?"

" Oh, you can take your choice."

" I can't have any young man from round the corner visiting us when you become Baroness von Katzenstein."

" I fancy there won't be many corners, or squares either, about your castle."

" You saucy girl ! Come, may I give you a canary ? Say yes."

" No ; I will never have another canary."

" Will you give me a kiss, then ?"

" Have you gone mad, Mr. Katzen ?' asked Abigail, in amazement.

" Only with love for you, my dear."

" You had better get sane, then, at once."

" Let me give you a kiss," he repeated, making a movement as if to come to her.

" Stay where you are," said Abigail determinedly, laying down her work and looking straight across the table at Mr. Katzen.

" Stay where I am, darling ! Why ?"

" Because, though I can take a joke as well as anybody, I am not going to take *that*."

" No ? Nor give it ?"

" Nor give it."

" We are very particular all of a sudden. Didn't we give one kiss, just one little one, to the donor of the dead canary ?"

" We did not."

" Or to our organist ?"

" No; or to the sexton, or the clerk, or the rector, or the policeman, or the sweep—there! As you will have it, I have never kissed a man, nor has any man ever kissed me, since my father died, and I was scarcely ten years old then. Kiss!" she added bitterly. "Who have I ever had to kiss me, or be kissed by me ?"

And with a strangled sob she took up her work again, and, though her eyes were full of tears, resumed her sewing.

It had been on the tip of Mr. Katzen's tongue to answer, " Here you have one most devoted, ready at this moment to kiss and be kissed ;" but he wisely refrained, and said :

" Tell me about your father, Abby; I have never heard you mention him before."

" There is nothing to tell," she answered.

" Talk, then," he urged, as if tenderly sympathetic; " it will relieve your heart. Who and what was he ?"

Miss Weir brushed the tears from her eyes and looked at Mr. Katzen, while a very demon of mischief seemed dancing about her face.

" He was poor, but honest," she said demurely.

" If honest, he would certainly remain poor," commented the Consul; " that goes without saying. But proceed, my Abigail— your narrative is charming."

" There is an end of it, at any rate," she replied.

" That can hardly be, when it is scarce begun," remarked Mr. Katzen. " Rather a case, perhaps, of 'hole in the ballad,' eh ? But never mind the hole — go on, fair maiden."

The fair maiden shook her head.

" Nothing more to go on with."

" Are you quite, quite certain ? For instance, did your papa, so poor, so honest, die comfortably in his bed ?"

Abigail looked at Mr. Katzen in surprise, then light dawned upon her.

" Oh, I understand," she said. " Whether my father died comfortably or not I cannot tell you ; but he died in his bed."

" Of what ?"

" Consumption, the doctors styled his disease," answered Abby. " Other people called it a broken heart."

" Heavens, child, what a gift you possess ! How you rivet my interest ! And your beloved mother—did she die of a broken heart too ?"

" That I cannot tell you."

" Her daughter, so beloved, was not beside her at the supreme moment ?"

Miss Weir worked steadily on as though she had not heard.

" Abigail," pleaded Mr. Katzen, " I am distracted with curiosity. Where were you when Providence saw fit—for our mutual benefit—to leave you an orphan ?"

" You have heard enough for one day—for many days," answered the girl, 'so provokingly that Mr. Katzen knew it was useless to try to pump her further.

" Not enough, but more than I have heard during all these long years. When we are one, my love, you will tell me everything ; you will keep no secret from your adoring Karl ?"

"When we are one, certainly not."

"You will even whisper to me the name of the present non-deserving young man?"

"What non-deserving young man?"

"The young man who does not seem to know what lips like yours were made for, the young man you go out to meet, and that you walk with sometimes."

It was an arrow shot at a venture, but it found the mark. All the colour faded out of Abigail's face, and then rushed back in a brilliant crimson tide that mantled cheeks and brow.

"Who told you that—who dared to tell you that?" she asked, her shield broken down for once.

"As for daring, my dear lofe, there is no law which hinders tongues wagging; and for the rest, if pretty girls will walk with men who are not their fathers, or grandfathers, or uncles, or brothers, wise people can only draw one inference——"

"Mr. Katzen," interrupted this pretty girl, "I insist upon your letting me know who it is that has said such a thing about me."

"You insist, do you? Say so again, darling—it fills me with rapture to see you so angry, so moved. Would I could fix that rich colour in your cheek! What rose might hope to surpass its damask!—but there, your look changes, it grows fierce almost. Calm yourself, sweet one, your wish shall be gratified. It was a little bird of the air, a tiny creature no bigger than my thumb, brought me the news."

" Pity it was not better employed," said Abigail.

" How could it have been better employed than in bringing tidings of the loved one to the lover ?"

" Mr. Katzen, I am getting tired of all this. You are not my lover."

" But I am, and you cannot alter that fact !"

" I am not in love with you, at all events."

" At present, perhaps not, the greater pity for me. It will come all in good time, though. I do not hurry you. Have out your foolish fancies, and your baby dreams, and after-

wards—but why that sudden movement,
what is wrong? Where is my beauty
going?"

"I do not know where *your* beauty may
be going, but as you cannot or will not talk
sense, *I* am going upstairs."

"Wait a moment—one moment, dear
Abby. Am I to be left here in sole charge,
with only the old clock for company, while I
wait the return of Mr. Brisco?"

"Mr. Brisco has not been out to-day," replied Abigail, "as you could have known
long ago, if you had taken the trouble to
inquire for him."

"And did I not inquire for him? Is it
possible? My faith, what an omission!
Come back, and forgive your Karl. No?
Ah! One day you will be sorry for the way
you are treating me. Never mind, I shall
not prove implacable. It is all the fault of
that naughty young man you meet when you
think nobody is looking. By-the-bye, what
is his name? I have forgotten it for the
moment."

"The same little bird who told you one

story must be quite able to tell you another,"
retorted Abigail. "Ask him, and do not
come here again troubling me, please."

" Never again ?"

" Never."

" It is impossible that you can mean that.
A nature so sweet——" But when he arrived
at this point, Abigail disappeared.

As he followed, in order to make his way
to Mr. Brisco's office, he heard the sound of
light young feet flying up the back staircase
to one of the smaller rooms in the old house.

" She runs well," he thought, " and there
is temper in her step. I have struck oil by
accident at last. She meets some one, and I
shall have to discover who it is. And now
for grim Old Mortality."

He knocked at the door of that narrow
apartment on the ground-floor previously
mentioned, and entered.

" Is that you, Mr. Katzen ?" said Mr.
Brisco, stretching out his hand with some
show of cordiality. The welcome was warmer
than usual, but the room cold. Involuntarily
the Consul shivered. The absence of all

signs of a fire seemed to intensify the misery
of a bleak, miserable winter's day. How
could that old man, with no blood in his
body, and no warm clothing on his back,
endure the temperature which tried Mr. Katzen, though his top-coat was thick and new,
and himself well nourished?

"You feel chilly, I am afraid?" remarked
Mr. Brisco.

"Not particularly," fibbed Mr. Katzen;
"only I come from a *tête-à-tête* with Miss
Weir, and after the warmth of her chamber
this atmosphere does not strike me as torrid.
Well—and how have you been this long
time?" he went on, anxious to avert the usual
remark he had learnt to know so well anent
the extravagance of large fires, of Abigail's
fatal fondness for too much heat, and the
modern craze of sitting moping over the
hearth instead of going out for a brisk
walk.

"See me," Mr. Brisco was wont to say by
way of brilliant and seductive example, "I
never feel cold. In the winter I sleep only
under one blanket. It is the rarest thing for

me to wear a top-coat. I do not indulge in stimulants, and where could you find a stronger man, or one who enjoys better health ?"

" As if life," thought Mr. Katzen, "were worth having on the terms. Could I suppose for one moment that when I get to be as old as Mr. Brisco, I should have to sit fireless and foodless, with a blue nose and numbed hands and an empty stomach, I would make at once for the next world by the nearest door."

" I don't believe you would," answered Mr. Bernberg, to whom he once made this remark. " I have a notion no world that lacks German beer and Rhine wine would tempt you across its frontier, my friend."

" How have you been this long time ? 'twere fitter to ask," said Mr. Brisco, in answer to the Consul's question. " It matters little how I am ; but for one rising and prospering like yourself, it matters a good deal."

" Yes, I am prospering," confessed Mr. Katzen modestly. " I find I shall make a big thing of my position."

" No one can be more glad to hear you say
so than I. It is very good of you to remember that such people as Abigail and myself
exist in this out-of-the-world spot."

" There is no spot which is so dear to me in
all the world as Botolph Lane, and no house
in Botolph Lane that seems so homelike as
this old mansion."

" Yet you never lived in it!" said Mr.
Brisco.

" I never slept in it, but live! Gott, if I
haven't lived here, I have lived nowhere!
How often has the snow lain in the court-
yard in my knowledge of the place; what
would I not now give to feel the sun of a
summer's afternoon burning my left shoulder,
as it used to do where I sat writing upstairs!
Was I not wont to watch the dingy trees in
St. Botolph's graveyard putting out fresh
leaves, clothing themselves again as in their
youth with tenderest, divinest green ; and
when the green departed, and the leaves grew
brown and dry, and dropped sadly to the
ground, did I not mourn with the trees, for
I felt the drear November days were at hand

when good fortune never seemed to remember me—never at all !"

Mr. Brisco did not answer. Perhaps through his mind also there passed at that moment a procession of the seasons he too had seen come and go since he entered the black and white marble hall, and took up his lonely life, keeping a door closed between himself and the world, of which the real door he locked and barred each night was but a symbol.

The years during which he dwelt apart had come and the years had gone, and what he had made of and felt in them was known so far but to God, for man could scarcely even guess at the struggling and miserable history they contained. He was not, however, in the habit of playing at the game of capping sentiment. If Mr. Katzen expected to seduce him into such a sport, he was greatly mistaken.

"At all events," he said, "good fortune seems now to have taken up her abode with you, though not here."

"But I want her with me here, where be-

fore she was always flit-flitting like a butter-
fly, but could scarce make up her mind to
settle. She seems a stranger to me in Mitre
Court. I have been thinking matters over.
I will take those two rooms most beautiful.
You will meet me in the rent."

" But," interposed Mr. Brisco, "what as
regards Mitre Court? You do not want to
have two places on your hands."

" Did I wish, I could let my present
offices to-morrow, and dispose of my posses-
sions at a fair profit," answered Mr. Katzen,
who understood his old landlord in many
respects thoroughly.

" You are a wonderful person," said Mr.
Brisco, half in doubt, half in admiration.

" But I do not want to get rid of them yet,
at all events till I can see how matters are
meaning to go. It may be I shall need
them as well as your offices, and more too.
Meantime, I desire worthy Sir Christopher's
dining and drawing-room. People would say
I was unwise to say this frankly, but you
are far too old a friend to take advantage
of my youth and inexperience. Now,

Mr. Brisco, in a word, what is your lowest figure ?"

" I am sorry," answered Mr. Brisco, but——"

"We agreed just now," interposed the New Andalusian Consul, "you were not to try and enhance their value. Surely you would not drive a hard bargain with your long tenant Katzen ?"

Mr. Brisco did not commit himself on this point ; he only said :

" Unfortunately, I have let the offices."

" Let the offices !—since when ?"

" The negotiation has been proceeding for some time, but the agreement was not signed till a fortnight ago."

" The offices are not occupied, though," persisted Mr. Katzen, who did not wish to believe the evidence of his ears.

" No ; the tenants do not enter into possession till the middle of December."

"Who are they ?"

" A firm of foreign wine merchants."

" I'd have you careful about your rent,' said Mr. Katzen, whose disbelief in the solvency of foreigners was almost as great as Mr. Jeffley's.

Mr. Brisco smiled ironically.

" I shall have my rent," he answered ; "it is guaranteed."

"Well, well," sighed the Consul, " I suppose I ought to be glad, but I feel disap·pointed. Still, I am glad; you stand in need of some good fortune, if anyone did. I hope it has come to you, too, at last."

" Think of all the time those offices have stood empty," said Mr. Brisco, declining the suggestion of comfort.

" That is true, that is what my friend Jeffley remarks—takes all the gilt off the gingerbread."

" Never much gilt at the best," added Mr. Brisco.

"You find it often confoundedly hard work to make the two ends meet, I should imagine."

" I have never complained, have I ?" retorted Mr. Brisco.

" No ; that makes it seem all the harder. Though I have said little, I have thought about you much. In fact, one reason why I called round to-day was to make a little proposition that would put a few pounds in your pocket."

" That is very kind of you."

" No, it is selfish. My plan was, if you could have let me those rooms, to ask a little personal help from you. I could not remunerate you perhaps quite as I ought, but ' little fish are sweet,' once again to quote the excellent Jeffley. It would have been more convenient, of course, if I had been on the premises, but, upon my honour, I don't see what is to prevent your coming to Mitre Court."

" There exists no physical impossibility about the matter, certainly," agreed Mr. Brisco, who sometimes liked to play an acquaintance as an angler plays a fish.

" Then come to me for a few hours each day," said Mr. Katzen eagerly. " We'll not quarrel about terms, I feel sure. It shall be what you like, salary—commission—anything !"

" But first tell me exactly what you mean,"

urged Mr. Brisco; "for example, 'a few hours a day'?"

" Just as long as you like."

" Very liberal on your part; still, I suppose, a phrase not to be too literally interpreted. I might like not to go at all; if so, what then?"

" Ah! you laugh," suggested Mr. Katzen.

" I am not laughing, indeed; be a little more explicit. For instance, at what time in the morning would it gratify you to see me?"

" I should try to suit your convenience— ten, shall we say?"

" Very well, say ten. Then, should you lock up the office, or would that duty devolve on me?"

" I am afraid, as a rule, I should have to ask you to lock up."

" About six?"

" Generally."

". Let us say six. Now, during the day when could I be off duty?"

" Mostly when I myself was in."

" You might find it difficult to say when that would be."

"Of course, I could not be quite exact. I am in sometimes for hours, and sometimes not for ten minutes."

"Yes."

"Virtually, you know, there is but little to do."

"Virtually, what you mean is that I should be your clerk."

"Surely such old friends need not put the matter in that way ?"

"Surely such old friends need not beat about the bush."

"I wanted to avoid giving umbrage."

"That was considerate, certainly. Still, Mr. Katzen, however much you choose to disguise the pill, it is there. You knew I should think it a pill, or you would not amiably have covered it with so much jam. If I took your pill, spite of all the jam, I should taste the bitter. If I had wanted a situation, do you think I am so infirm, mentally or physically, I could not have obtained one long ago ?"

"I make no doubt you could have obtained one," admitted Mr. Katzen, "though why you did not wish to increase your income by obtaining it, baffles me."

Mr. Brisco smiled, not pleasantly.

"You do not read your Bible as attentively as you do the newspaper, I am afraid," he said, "or you would remember that Solomon states positively, 'Better is a dry morsel and quietness therewith, than an house full of sacrifices with strife.' Solomon was a very wise man."

"Faith! I think I'd rather take my chance with the sacrifices than the dry morsel," retorted Mr. Katzen.

"I dare say you would—I think it's extremely likely you would," said Mr. Brisco, so nastily that Mr. Katzen thought it expedient to retreat as soon as he could without rudeness.

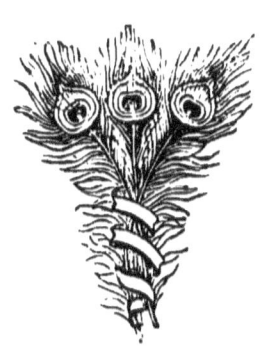

CHAPTER VIII.

THE TIDE TURNS.

AVING parted on such terms, Mr. Katzen, who meanwhile had triumphantly got rid of his clerk, felt considerably surprised to see Mr. Brisco walk into his office early the next morning.

"He has thought better of it," he considered, "or perhaps the new party has cried off about the rooms."

"Sit down, sit down, Mr. Brisco," he said aloud; "I shall be at leisure in a minute. Look at the *Times.*"

Mr. Brisco accepted the offer, and for a while silence reigned, broken only by the swift movement of Mr. Katzen's paper-knife as he cut open his letters, and then by the crackle caused by rapidly turning the sides. At length he finished.

" Now, Mr. Brisco !" he exclaimed cheerily, " to what fortunate chance am I indebted for the honour of this visit ?"

" In the first place," was the answer, " I come to apologize. I really believe you meant well by me yesterday."

" And to myself," added Mr. Katzen.

" I think your offer was a mistake. I think all such offers are mistakes ; but I lay no claim to infallibility."

" Surely that cannot be," said the Consul, and he grinned.

" Perhaps," admitted Mr. Brisco, smiling in spite of himself; "we none of us know ourselves."

Mr. Katzen thought he knew himself pretty well, but he did not say so.

" I do not want a situation, if only for this reason," went on Mr. Brisco—" the man has still to be born with whom I could agree, w ere I servant and he master. But, as I re-marked before, I believe you meant your

offer in good faith, and I ought not perhaps
to have been so curt over it."

"Be sure I took no offence. It is long
since I understood you," answered Mr. Katzen. "You have a right to your own notions.
Who should know your affairs and feelings as
well as yourself? I had best say no more
on the subject, because, were I to tell you
what passed through my mind besides my
personal advantage when I made the suggestion, I should run the risk of angering you
again."

"Yes, I fancy we had better drop the
matter," replied Mr. Brisco. "Now I have
come to ask your advice, you will not refuse
it, though I was a churl yesterday."

"I deny the 'churl,' but let that pass.
How can my poor advice serve you?"

"A friend, a—a person I know, is anxious
to make a little money."

"Heavens! He does not stand alone—
but I interrupt you."

"Some time since, he bought a small
property—not to trouble you with too many
details—that is likely to eat into the bulk of

his available capital, and now what he wants is to utilize the trifle that will remain—to turn it to the best account."

" How much has he to spare ?"

" A few—a very few hundred pounds."

" Which must not be lost ?"

" Exactly."

" Then he can do nothing speculative ; and it puzzles me to imagine how under such circumstances a fortune is to be made. In love and war, and commerce, ' Nothing venture, nothing have,' holds true."

" But you, Mr. Katzen, have managed to make money ?"

" Not much, so far."

" You have been able, at all events, to keep moving, and deny yourself very little you desire."

" I ! Why, I have had nothing as yet I desired. It is true I have had the mere necessaries of life, because I am not a person to do without my dinner, so long as a dinner can be got for cash or credit ; besides, I have always been venturing, and my ventures brought me into connection with people who

put good little trifles in my way. I always
keep moving—if I am not fishing I am
mending my net."

" Then you think nothing is to be gained
without risk ?"

" Very little."

" Yet some men do grow rich without
running risks."

" I know how that is done too. With
much interest I have watched the rise and
progress of good, steady young men—men
who at twenty have old heads on their
shoulders—who determine to get on, and
who do get on. A young man of this sort, for
example, saves and stints in cheap lodgings ;
he takes no pleasure ; he insures his life ;
he subscribes to a building society. He
marries some plain, managing woman, whose
papa endows her with perhaps a thousand
pounds. Money makes money, you know.
After a while people begin to mention him as
a very successful man—so he is ; but I fancy
if we came to cast up the price he has paid for
it, we should think the cost somewhat exces-
sive. I should, for sure. Unless there is

some enjoyment to be got out of money
while one is making it, I can't see the good
of it. Do you think I would do without my
chop to-day for any amount of venison when
I am toothless ? No, we must work with an
eye to the future, doubtless ; but it is worse
than folly to ill-treat the good present, which
is all we can lay our hands on, for the sake of
what may never come."

"There may be something in what you
say," agreed Mr. Brisco coldly, " but still it
seems to me no person having so small a
sum of money as the individual I mentioned
would be justified in risking its loss."

"It is a matter of temperament. He
would consider the loss as a very serious
affair, no doubt."

" Of that there can be no question."

" Then clearly he is not one who should
speculate."

" I should say he should not speculate—
loss would almost break his heart ; but I did
not know—I live so apart from the world of
business. I thought possibly there were safe
and profitable investments out of which a

man so situated might improve his position."

"As for investments, there are plenty. The Three per Cents, mortgage on freehold land, good ground-rents."

Mr. Brisco smiled.

" That is scarcely what I meant."

" What did you mean ?" asked Mr. Katzen, with an excellent affectation of ignorance.

" I meant that occasionally you, who are always about, might hear of some chance where the investment of a small amount for a short period would return a good percentage."

Mr. Katzen shook his head.

" High percentage means, you know, as a rule, bad security—but stay," he added, " a few pounds can now and then be made in Consols, and they are thought safe enough."

" For that it would be necessary to employ a broker."

" Yes ; but I don't know that your friend could expect any broker to watch the market for him. Without that, he might not even make an eighth per cent. per annum. I

judge, from what you say, he is a bit of a
duffer, a fellow who knows nothing about the
dodges of The House."

" It is not a flattering portrait, but probably
a likeness. And you think you can do nothing
to help him. Of course, any small commission you felt you could accept would be at
your service."

" Commission, pah ! do you suppose I am
all business—all brass and iron ? It would
only be great pleasure to me if I could put
your friend in the way of making a little fortune ; but at the minute I fail to see—stop,
though; wait a little, give me time to consider
myself."

Since no objection could be raised by anyone to this proceeding, Mr. Katzen put both
hands to his forehead, and for a while sat
considering himself. At last he looked up :

" Is there any pressing hurry about this,
Mr. Brisco ?" he asked. " Does your friend
want to see a return to-morrow or the next
day, or can he wait a little ?"

" That would depend on how long the wait
was likely to last."

" Well, now, I tell you what we'll do. I
am acquainted with a broker, a queer sort of
a fellow, but sharp—sharp like to a needle.
This sort of thing is not much in his way—
as a rule he only attends to matters like to
leave him a decent margin ; but he knows me
well, and I have, I may say, been able to
serve him to a small extent in my little way.
He will do what I ask."

" But pray remember that I should not
wish you to put yourself under an obligation."

" It is no obligation, and if it were, do you
think I should mind laying myself under one
for my own advantage, or for the advantage
of a friend ?   Besides, he knows he will lose
nothing by doing me a good turn.   I am
going to be so big a man soon—I shall be
able to serve many people.   This friend of
yours, has he the money available, or must
he stop to realize——"

" It is available now."

" Then you bring me a hundred pounds,
that will be plenty to begin with ; and if at the
end of a month he is satisfied with the re-

turns, he can go in for more. If the thing is to be done at all, it can only be done by constantly turning the amount. A friend, a countryman of mine, netted a hundred and fifty pounds in a fortnight by just watching the market—pretty tidy on five hundred pounds, eh ?—but he never ran a risk, never ran the risk even of loss of gain. If it was only a sixteenth profit that could be made, he sold."

" He went on, I suppose, till he amassed a fortune ?"

" He went on and made a fortune, then he grew too venturesome and lost every cent. Ah, it was a thousand pities ! Man with a wife and young family too."

" Shall I find you here at two o'clock ? I could bring the amount then, if not troubling you too much," said Mr. Brisco, who never seemed to think it necessary even to feign an interest in anyone but himself.

" Trouble ! do not talk of trouble, please. As for two o'clock—let me see," and Mr. Katzen took out his watch and went into an elaborate calculation, which finally justified

him in saying he would be found in Mitre
Court at two sharp. "Make it as near that
time as you can, will you kindly?" he added,
and then he walked with Mr. Brisco out on
to the landing, and bade him take care of
the stairs. "They are not so good as those
in Botolph Lane," he finished; after which
statement he re-entered his room and closed
the door.

"I must not be too sure," he soliloquized,
"or I should think, Karl, Heaven had a
favour unto you. I hope his friend won't
raise any foolish objections. Suppose now,
only suppose, either of them guessed my
whole worldly wealth at this minute consists
of two-and-twenty shillings—I wonder how
long they would keep that hundred pounds
before letting me handle a penny of it? A
long time, I have a notion."

Punctually at two o'clock the money came.
Mr. Katzen gave Mr. Brisco a receipt for it,
and the business was concluded.

"Now, Mrs. Jeffley," decided the Consul,
"we will pay that rum-drinking, profane-
swearing old ruffian of a Captain Hassell.

You are at heart a spiteful cat, and you have shown your claws more than once lately. You would talk, too, if the fit took you. Yes, we will pay the Captain ;" and he sighed as he put the fair crisp notes in his pocket-book ere sticking a notice on his door, " Return immediately," and making his way to the bank, the manager and clerks of which held him in much contempt, never dreaming he was destined to astonish them very greatly in a not remote future.

As matters turned out, he did not repay Mrs. Jeffley. He offered her the money, but she refused to accept it.

" I have settled with the Captain," she said, waving the money aside. " I thought it better to be done with him, and I do not want the amount at present. Keep it, if it is of any use to you ; I shall not need it till after Christmas, anyhow."

" I can easily spare it," coquetted Mr. Katzen. " I brought it home with me on purpose to pay you. Come, Mrs. Jeffley ; ' short accounts,' you know, as your husband says, ' make long friends.' "

"We have been long friends," she answered, "and sometimes our accounts have not been very short, either. I wish you would keep it; do, or I shall think you are offended because I was a little put out the night before last."

"No, upon my good conscience!" declared Mr. Katzen.

"First there's one thing, and then there's another," mourned the brisk Maria. "What with the servants, and what with the children, and what with the lodgers, I often think life's not worth the having."

"But, my dear soul——"

"Yes, yes, Mr. Katzen, that's all very well; but even you are often not like what you used to be. It is natural people should be taken up with their own concerns, and no doubt you must have a deal on your mind. I can make allowances. What hurts me is, nobody makes allowances for me."

"My kind friend—my best of friends——"

"No, don't," interrupted Mrs. Jeffley, releasing her plump hand, of which, in the ardour of his gratitude, Mr. Katzen had possessed himself. "Anything I have done, I have been glad to do. I'd have done more, had it lain in my power. I want no thanks, only don't take me up wrong if I speak a bit short. We have all our troubles. I have mine, little as you may think it."

"Mrs. Jeffley," said her friend, "I do think it. Who should know better than I where the shoe that looks so neat and easy pinches? If I do not speak, I feel; but what have I done that you should misjudge *me*? what have I left undone? Even this money! it was short notice, you know; yet here I bring the full tale that you may be put to no inconvenience with the impatient Captain. You were not visible when I went out yesterday morning—worn out, exhausted, as Mrs. Childs told me—you were with your child last night again. This morning I could not see you, to tell you to be no more anxious; and now here is the amount. What could I do more? What else were it fitting I should have done?"

"Oh, I can't say, I am sure. Only just keep it for the present to please me. I am

so upset altogether, I scarce know whether I
am talking sense or nonsense. You wouldn't
vex me more than I am vexed, would you,
Mr. Katzen ?"

"If you put it that way," he answered,
reluctantly withdrawing the money.

"I do put it that way. When you want us
to be quits I feel just like losing everybody."

"Heaven knows I would be the last to
make you feel just like that."

"I used to think so—I did indeed," answered
Mrs. Jeffley almost tearfully.

"Well, you may think so still ; and to show
you I am not in the least changed, I will
keep this money, and thank you for your
trust in me."

"Trust, what an idea! And now I will
bid you good-night. The child must be
wanting me."

"Good-night ; and, Mrs. Jeffley, do get to
bed. You will kill yourself if you go on as
you are doing, resting never."

"And if I did kill myself, nobody would
care."

"Now, now, now," remonstrated Mr. Katzen. "After a sound sleep you will look on life with different eyes. See, I put up your loan. Güte Nacht, Geliebte." Into which sentence—which Mrs. Jeffley understood but imperfectly, and only at all, indeed, from the fact that she had heard it repeated many times before on occasions like the present— Mr. Katzen contrived to throw such an amount of respectful adoration that Mrs. Jeffley, in an access of alarmed, if mistaken, modesty, deemed it advisable to terminate the interview and ascend to the room where " Billy" was crying for her.

In the solitude of his chamber Mr. Katzen's thoughts did not run perhaps on the track his "loved friend" imagined. He considered first that things were going fortunately for him—that Heaven evidently did mean to favour him : that Fortune was relenting, that Fate certainly did intend the New Andalusian loan to make one great splash, or else Fate really could not know its own mind; that it was a pity he had not secured those other few hundreds belonging to Mr. Brisco's friend. Only it was possible in asking too

much he might have ruined all—seeming too
eager, he might get nothing; that if Jack
Jeffley had not been promoted and so thrown
his wife's " excellent temper out of gear," she
would not have been so ready to repay
Captain Hassell out of her own pocket. " It
is always one scale down, the other scale up,
with the dear woman," he finished. " Well,
we shall see what we can make out of this
windfall. By the way, I much marvel who
Brisco's friend may be! I thought he never
had a friend at all."

This was a matter which had not before
occurred to Mr. Katzen. Now he did catch
sight of it, he felt bound to run the quarry to
earth. Walking up and down his room, he
considered the question. He smoked two
cigarettes over it. He ran back to the time
when he first went to Botolph Lane—he
recalled the incidents connected with his
sojourn there—he taxed his memory to bring
back the form of any man likely or unlikely
to come under the category of " friend" to
Mr. Brisco, unavailingly.

Next to his love of speculative intrigue,

Mr. Katzen's strongest passion perhaps was patient and curious analysis. He knew he should never be able to rest now till he had solved the mystery of this mysterious individual possessed of a very few hundred pounds. Could he have any connection with Abigail ? Were the two strange incidents of a starving stray and a moneyed friend connected together ? The Consul folded his dressing-gown more closely around his person, flung away the remaining inch of his cigarette, threw himself into an armchair drawn close before the fire, and thought. He thought thus for best part of an hour—thought till at last a gratified smile stole slowly over his face.

"Yes, I fancy that is it, Karl," he said meditatively, as he stirred the coals into a fitful blaze. "And you have always suspected something of the sort."

CHAPTER IX.

CHRISTMAS had gone. Not so the cold introduced by Wilhelmina into Fowkes' Buildings. Every creature in Mrs. Jeffley's house, from the latest lodger and last domestic to the youngest child, had been afflicted with cough, sore throat, or some analogous malady.

"To the devil with such a climate!" said Mr. Katzen. He had sneezed fifteen times in succession, and a black London fog pervaded the whole building. The gas was blinking as if drunk, which is a way gas often has in one's extremest need; so perhaps Mr. Katzen might be excused an aspiration, hard certainly on a land which had neither asked nor desired the pleasure or his presence. " I shall go down to Brighton by first train to-morrow morning. I can't stand this any longer."

" Lucky to be you, who can go where you like, when you like, and stay as long as you like," answered Frank Scott, to whom Mr. Katzen's remark had been addressed. Scott himself was going about his business with an inflamed eye and a gumboil.

" You might have been lucky too, if you had seen fit to take my offer, instead of sticking with your bill-broking friend in Nicholas Lane," retorted the Consul, who as yet was ignorant of the young man's rise in the world.

Frank had decided not to blazon forth his good fortune to Mr. Jeffley's typical Dick, Tom, and Harry—and for once Jack, entreated to preserve the secret, had managed to do so.

Frank smiled, as well as a man suffering under such physical difficulties could smile.

" Even if I had availed myself of your

kind offer, Mr. Katzen," he said, " I fancy you would have expected *me* to stay in Mitre Court while *you* went to Brighton."

" Perhaps I might," answered Mr. Katzen, laughing ; " indeed, I know I should ; still, if you had taken my well-meant offer, I would have shown you ways to make money enough to become your own master. As it is, you will go on run-running about the town in order to make money for another man till your head is white."

" White with age, not sin, I hope."

" Bah, there is no sin but poverty. Let the priests talk as they will, that is the only unpardonable crime nowadays. Personally, dear young man," went on Mr. Katzen, " I am not so sorry you thought it better to stay with Brintolf than come with me, as perhaps I ought. I have now a first-rate clerk, one not as you only owning one tongue. He is the master of many languages. He can talk Spanish, Portuguese, jabber to anyone, any-where. Ah ! Rothsattel is a clever fellow ; I had a find in him !"

" I rejoice to hear you are so well suited,"

said Frank, with a smile which Mr. Jeffley would have called "dubious."

"I should be right enough as regards everything," answered Mr. Katzen, "if I were only rid of this confounded cold."

"You have not as bad a cold as Mr. Jeffley," remarked young Scott, administering the sort of consolation usually considered so excellent.

"The fact that his is bad makes not mine any better," said Mr. Katzen. "Though, faith! it is a good joke to see the big man take on as he does about a quinsy."

"If you had quinsy, Mr. Katzen, I fancy you would not think it much of a joke."

"I hope I should bear it better than our friend. He imagines he is going to die, I believe."

If anything, this was rather understating the case. Jack not merely imagined his hour had come, but felt sure it had. Personal illness and he were almost strangers; and now, stricken and well-nigh starved, he bemoaned his fate to all and any he could find to listen to him.

Mrs. Jeffley refused to listen; when he tried to enlist her sympathy and arouse her anxiety she snubbed him into silence.

" Die !" she repeated ; " what would you die of ? Quinsy—pack of rubbish ! People like you don't die so easily ; it would take a lot to kill you, I know. You are nothing but a great baby. Why, Bertie would be ashamed to grizzle the way you are doing. Just think of Sydney, poor lamb ! when he cut his finger to the bone, and the blood was streaming down his pinafore in torrents, he never opened his lips. As for you, you never shut them, wanting this, that, and the other, as if I had nothing on earth to do but consider your likings and dislikings."

" I hope you won't be sorry for all this some day," remonstrated Jack. " Some day when I am dead and gone——"

" What should I be sorry for ?" asked Mrs. Jeffley. " That I am not so foolish as you ? If I were, I don't know what would become of us. Here you have been three whole weeks without doing one stroke of work, and all because you would persist in leaving off that thick wrapper one day the sun chanced to show himself for about five minutes."

"Well, well, perhaps it was my own fault; but I have been terribly punished."

"Not a bit of it. *I* have been punished; I have had to attend to you hand and foot, early and late, night and day. I am sure, as Mrs. Childs says——"

"If you tell me another word she says, or send her to me with any more of her vile messes, I won't be answerable for the consequences. There will be murder done, Maria, and by me."

"Dear, dear, nobody can please you!"

"It is not easy to be pleased with no food in my stomach, and a thing like a mangel-wurzel stopping up my throat. I shall send for another doctor. It is no use sitting quietly till death fetches me, without making one effort for life."

"I wouldn't make a laughing-stock of myself," answered Mrs. Jeffley. "If Dr. Morris can't cure you, nobody can."

"I am not so sure of that."

"Well, I am," retorted his wife, "and that's enough."

Jack considered this a harsh way of putting matters, but facts justified if they did not soften Mrs. Jeffley's statement. That night the lump which Jack had indeed believed to be as large as a mangel-wurzel, broke, as the doctor said, "beautifully."

Then indeed Jack felt his hour had come, and braced himself up to meet the inevitable —when sick, faint, weak and dazed, he laid his head back on the pillows, he honestly believed he should never raise it again.

"You feel all right now," said the doctor in a disgustingly cheerful tone, but Jack was incapable of dissent.

"What you want is food, not physic," went on his medical adviser; "but we must not overdo it—we must be careful."

Again Jack made no answer; the world seemed slipping away from him. Deedes' was a mere memory far back almost as boyhood. The time was past when he longed for beef-tea and could have devoured jelly. His youngest child had more strength than he ; all he desired was to be let alone—to be left in quiet while he passed to that bourne he had been so dreading to reach.

" Your husband is very much pulled down," said the doctor to Mrs. Jeffley, as he stood in the passage, holding his hat in his left hand while he carefully smoothed the nap round and round with the right.

" The wonder would be if he wasn't," answered Mrs. Jeffley. " A strong hearty man used to his four regular meals a day, taking nothing for all this time—enough to pull him down."

" He will require great care."

" He can have no better care than he has had. It was not my fault that he would not force himself to swallow."

The doctor knew better than to enter upon any controversy connected with so vexed a question, one which had indeed previously been threshed out as completely as any question could be with Mrs. Jeffley.

" Our patient is very low and weak," he remarked.

" I don't need anybody to tell me that,"

answered "our patient's" wife. "When people once begin to give up and to let themselves down, it is hard to say where they may end."

"But with your good nursing and his own excellent constitution I trust he will pull round rapidly," went on the doctor, as though in continuation of his former sentence; "still he must not play any tricks with himself. If it were not for the excellent care I know you take of him, I should feel more uneasy than I do. I need not tell *you*, it is always with these strong, hearty men we have the most trouble. They have a nasty knack sometimes of collapsing in an unaccountable way."

"Do you mean, doctor, that my husband is in any—any—*danger?*" asked Mrs. Jeffley.

"No—no—nothing of the sort, only he is very low—it is well to be on the safe side—that is all, and I shall look in early to-morrow."

"Now what can the man's notion be?" considered Mrs. Jeffley. "He does not imagine, I hope, that Jack is neglected, or that he wants for anything money can buy. I am sure if he had fancied molten gold I'd have tried to get it for him hot from the Mint."

She turned into Jack's little parlour for some trifle she required ere going upstairs and the cold, uninhabited, formal look of the room struck her with an unpleasant chill.

Nothing there now to find fault with— no slippers lying about, no newspaper tossed aside, no book left open, no fireirons at other than the correct angle. Supposing, just supposing for a moment the parlour were in the same formal state of neatness as then obtained, only that instead of the table another ornament occupied the centre of the carpet.

The vision came before her eyes with perfect distinctness—trestles supporting a coffin—and Jack, with all his worrying crotchets and useless old-fashioned notions, out of the way for ever.

Mrs. Jeffley was not a person who could strictly be termed imaginative. Indeed, when speaking subsequently of the matter—

which she did not do, however, for a long long
time—she declared she could not think what
possessed her, whatever could have put such
a notion in her mind ; yet undoubtedly fancy
did play the extraordinary trick of showing
her not only a few of the terrors that follow
in the wake of death, but of reviving from
out the past some memory of Jack as she
used to think of him before it dawned upon
her comprehension how foolish he was, and
how far inferior to herself.

The whole thing did not occupy longer
than the time a man might dip his head in a
bucket of water and draw it out again. Yet
it seemed so real, and carried Mrs. Jeffley so
far from her immediate surroundings, that
she quite started when a voice inquired :

" Is there anything more, 'm, you'll require
before I go ?   Because, if there is, I am sure
I'll wait with pleasure."

Mrs. Jeffley turned like one dazed, and
beheld Mrs. Childs, whose face having
swelled, the " one grace she lacked," to quote
Mr. Katzen, had now been added.

" Lor, 'm !" exclaimed that excellent woman

ere Mrs. Jeffley could frame a reply to her question, "aren't you well? You give me quite a turn. If you'd seen a ghost, 'm, you couldn't be whiter."

"Ghost enough, I think, to have people come frightening one as you frightened me," retorted Mrs. Jeffley. "I had no idea any person was behind me. Why did you not make some noise?"

"I knocked three times, 'm, and coughed twice; and then, seeing you were wropped in thought, I made so free at last as to speak. If I'd thought I should frighten you I would have bitten my tongue out first—you know I would, 'm."

"I know nothing of the sort," answered Mrs. Jeffley, glad of any whipping-boy on whom she could vent her irritation. "Did you take the coals upstairs as I asked you?"

"Yes, 'm; and I caught a glance at master. How bad he do look, to be sure!"

"Nonsense! the doctor says he is going on as well as possible."

"I am sure I am glad to hear it, 'm; not as it is always best to depend on doctors, as

34—2

witness my sister's husband's father, you may
call to mind I told you about, 'm—died
without making a will, all because the first
surgeons said he was good for another twenty
years, and him all the time dying before their
very eyes."

"I do not want to hear anything more
about your brother-in-law's father—you have
told me the whole affair over and over again,"
said Mrs. Jeffley, not merely rudely but
unfairly, since Mrs. Childs was scarcely in a
position to answer her back. "And as for
Mr. Jeffley, I believe what Dr. Morris tells
me, and I do not intend to believe anyone
else."

"That is a great comfort to know, 'm,"
replied Mrs. Childs, who was an expert at
paying her debts in malt when she felt afraid
of discharging them in meal. "I am foolish,
I'm aware ; but as I came downstairs the poor
dear master's white sunk face seemed to
haunt me, and I could not help thinking to
myself, 'Missus *has* been a fortunate woman ;
not a bit more fortunate, though, than she
deserves—as I have right to say, none better.

She has never lost chick nor child, nor had a
bad illness herself, hard as she has worked,
with her mind always busy about something ;
but now, oh dear ! if it should be the Lord's
will to take Mr. Jeffley, what would she do ?
—left all alone with a young family, and
deprived of a husband who never crossed her
in anythink, and fairly worshipped the ground
she walked on.' It all came upon me at
once," finished Mrs. Childs, applying the
corner of her black shawl to her face, which
was only a degree less black, "as I came
down the stairs I have been up so often
—it seemed as if there was a spell on
me."

"I wish you would not talk such folly,"
said Mrs. Jeffley impatiently. "Mr. Jeffley
is not going to die—he is getting well as fast
as he can. No," went on Mrs. Childs's
mistress hurriedly, with a view of cutting
short any further remarks the estimable
woman might feel disposed to indulge in,
"nothing more will be required to-night.
You need not stop any longer."

But still Mrs. Childs lingered.

"Has the poor master got his medicine, 'm?" she asked.

"No; but Dr. Morris will send it round directly."

"And are you sure, 'm, you wouldn't like me to stay here, in case anything should be wanted of a sudden, or anyone fetched? You'll excuse me, 'm, but I can't abear the notion of your being left all by yourself. If the master should be took worse, what could you do?"

"I'd do very well," answered Mrs. Jeffley; "there are plenty of people in the house I could call up in a minute."

"Of course, 'm, you know best, and you are very brave; still, I'd like well to stop. I could just run home and have a bite of supper, and come back, if you would let me. It would be no hardship to me, 'm, sitting up."

"There is no need for anybody to sit up," declared Mrs. Jeffley. "To hear you talk, one would think my husband was dying."

"Lord send it may not come to that!" ejaculated Mrs. Childs piously. "Well, 'm, wishing you good-night, and the master better."

" Good-night," said Mrs. Jeffley brusquely, in a tone intended to assure her henchwoman that whatever happened to Mr. Jeffley, she, Maria, would rise equal to the occasion.

"She's as hard as steel," remarked Mrs. Childs to Sophia the while the pair partook of toasted cheese, which Mrs. Childs felt was the only thing on that particular evening she could "let inside her lips;" "but I'm sure I touched her. If he does die—and he looks as like death as a man can, not laid out for his coffin—she'll soon find out the difference."

" Yes, she'll find the difference," agreed Sophia, speaking with her mouth full.

" If he should go," said Mrs. Childs, the " he" referring to Mr. Jeffley, "she can't be off giving me a full suit of black."

" No, she can't be off of giving you a full suit," capped Sophia.

This was the sort of conversation which pleased Mrs. Childs when she could permit herself to unbend, precisely as a swinging waltz air sometimes proves agreeable to the disciples of Wagner after one of The Master's most stupendous effects.

As if he had known the precise end to which Mrs. Childs' wishes were tending, and took a pleasure in frustrating them, Mr. Jeffley, so far from making haste to " be laid out for his coffin," proceeded to get well surely, if somewhat slowly.

That he did not make headway so fast as could have been desired might be traced to two causes : one, he, a strong man, had been brought by compulsory starvation almost within sight of the gates of death ; the other——

"You have something on your mind," affirmed the doctor one day, when Jack's languor, contrasted with Jack's pulse, puzzled him exceedingly.

" I have ; though I don't know how you found that out," replied Mr. Jeffley. " But I mean to get it off my mind the first day I am allowed to leave the house."

" How far do you want to go ?" asked the doctor, who was accustomed to prescribe for sane people, and knew how good it is sometimes to talk common-sense even to the grievously sick.

"Only into the City—to Throgmorton Street."

"And to stop for how long?"

"Say half an hour at the outside."

"Talking all the time?"

"Lord, no—I should hope not; talking, say, three minutes. I only want to buy in some stock."

"You are quite sure—you are not going to excite yourself about anything?"

"I am only going to do what I tell you."

"Then the sooner you get the matter off your mind the better. Wrap yourself up well, take a cab—four-wheeler—do not stop longer than you can help, and I dare say I shall find you none the worse to-morrow."

"Do you mean that I may venture out to-day?" asked Jack incredulously.

"Certainly, there is nothing deadly wrong with you now;" which Jack felt to be a very hard statement, believing, as he honestly did, no one had ever been so ill before.

"Why, it is a trouble to me to lift my hand to my head," he was wont to declare.

He returned home about four; arriving tired enough in Fowkes' Buildings at what Mrs. Childs called the "slackest" time of the day.

It was she who, spite of his previous expostulation, brought him beef-tea and a glass of wine, explaining, "Poor missus had laid herself down to see if she could close her eyes for a few minutes; but I'll tell her you're back, sir, if you would wish me to do so," in a tone which seemed to add the words, "and a brute you would be if you wished anything of the sort."

Mr. Jeffley answered that he would not have his wife disturbed for the world; then, finishing his beef-tea, he said he wanted nothing more, and lay down on the sofa to think in the firelight.

The events of the nine previous months supplied him with abundant matter for reflection.

"It never rains but it pours," says the old proverb; and by means of what seemed to

his simple mind a perfect deluge of incidents,
Mr. John Jeffley had proved that the old
proverb embodied a simple truth.

First came to him the amazing knowledge
of Mr. Gregson's wickedness. Though he
never liked Mr. Gregson—the manager
having been always too high and mighty, too
much of a "stand-off-a-little-further-if-you-
please, and keep-your-distance-my-good-fel-
low sort of gentleman" to please honest,
simple Jack—he had nevertheless believed in
the *bona fides* of that enterprising individual.
When that shock was a little what he called
"overgot," he felt able to devote his mind to
the surprising fact that Frank Scott, "of all
people in the world," had discovered Mr.
Gregson's game and checkmated it.

"I always thought and I always said,"
considered Mr. Jeffley, "that young Scott
had more in him than anybody imagined, but
it never did enter into my head that he would
have had the 'nous' to unravel a skein of
this sort. It must be the German, I suppose,
teaches a man to rise up early enough to
understand such goings on as Gregson's. I

wonder now, if anybody had taught me to speak that unchristian lingo, whether I should have got through the world better ;" and Jack smoked many pipes while he argued out this knotty point, which involved a more important issue, namely, whether he ought to speculate in having some one to give the " young ones" lessons in a language he firmly believed had been invented by the devil.

Finally, as was natural, he decided against letting any child belonging to him have anything to do with a tongue which must, according to his creed, have come from— well, it is unnecessary to be too precise about the locality.

" If they can't get along with plain English," he thought, " they may just as well not try to get on at all. It would seem to me a sort of disgrace to my father's memory if I heard a child of mine jabbering to any —— foreigners in their own tongue, which can't seem so bad to them or they'd never go on cracking their jaws over it as they do. I don't understand how Scott, not five-and-twenty years old yet, learnt to read and to talk like so many of

them as he does. I can see he's a bit
ashamed of it, and no wonder ; seems afraid,
when he has to interpret, to speak up hearty.
Well, that's to his credit anyhow ; and I am
sure, however he got his knowledge, it was
honestly. I only hope this quick promotion
won't turn his head—and for that matter,
Jack, I do trust you mayn't begin to think
too much of yourself. Manager of Deedes' !
Oh, dear me, if my poor old mother could
only have lived, how proud she'd be ! But
she's better off, I'm sure—the last time I saw
her living she had failed greatly, and her
rheumatism was very bad."

These events, which all meant good in
some way to Mr. John Jeffley, having thus
occurred, and thus been partly digested, Fate,
who about this particular time chanced to be
in a most benignant mood, could not resist
flinging another piece of good fortune towards
the man she had never before thought worth
considering.

"I say, Frank," cried Mr. Jeffley one
afternoon, bursting open the door of Sir
Christopher's dining-room in Botolph Lane,

"what do you think has happened now? My old godmother, that never gave me as much as a teething-ring, and who I'm sure I thought was dead twenty years ago, has just quitted this wicked world and left to her beloved godson, John Jeffley—that's me, you know—fifteen hundred pounds in Consols— fifteen hundred pounds!—as I am a living sinner."

"I congratulate you with all my heart."

"What had I best do with it? Come now, advise me."

Frank Scott looked straight in Jack's handsome, eager face—looked, seemed inclined to speak, then thought better of the matter, and held his tongue.

"Why don't you answer me?" asked Mr. Jeffley.

"I am afraid of giving offence."

"I can't think what has come to you lately," said Jack. "You've never been a bit like yourself since that night we went up to Hamilton Place. How could you offend me? Am I so apt to take offence? Come, what were you going to advise?—out with it."

"I was going to advise you not to tell your wife," answered Frank, looking away from Mr. Jeffley as he spoke.

If he had glanced towards him he would have seen the colour mount higher and higher in Jack's face.

"I don't want to hurt you, but it is true— for you have told me so yourself—that you have not been able to put a halfpenny by; and you know as well as I do, if Mrs. Jeffley knows of this legacy, at the end of a year it will all be gone. She would take another house, or refurnish, or do something of the sort. She would not squander the money, but all the same it would go; and if you think your position over you must see, with your family, you have no right to let such a sum of money slip through your fingers."

Mr. Jeffley did not say a word. He stood for a moment utterly silent, then walked to the door. Frank followed this movement with his eyes. He felt sorry, though not surprised; the usual fate of counsellors was his.

Jack slowly turned the handle, opened the

door, went out, closed the door behind him. Frank remained standing, a pained look on his face and a heavier pain at his heart. He was fond of this foolish husband, and——

Once again the door opened, and Jack appeared. He walked straight across the room and held out his hand.

" I know you did not mean to vex me, old fellow," he said huskily; and then he went.

This conversation took place just after Christmas, and proved a sore trouble to Mr. Jeffley. It seemed to him an act well-nigh of disloyalty to keep such a secret from his wife; to him it was as natural to tell, as many persons find it to withhold. There were no dark corners in his nature; if there had been, it may be his wife would have liked him better. To the unsophisticated female there is always something attractive about mystery, even if it be the mystery of wickedness. Eve would never have eaten of the apple if she had not believed there lurked in it somewhere a pleasant flavour of sin.

Jack was the sort of man who could have gone through life perfectly contented if

allowed to do his daily work in peace, and
return every evening to a quiet home, where,
seated beside a clean hearth and a bright
fire, he could have told his wife the few
experiences which had come to him since
morning, the while she darned his socks or
mended the children's dresses.

If Heaven had seen fit to give him such
increase of prosperity as might justify a four-
wheeled trap and a stout cob, he would have
enjoyed driving his missus and the young
ones out to the Forest on summer evenings
more than words could tell.

His ideal of a perfect existence was a fat
farm in some one of the home counties, with
an orchard near the house and a stream
meandering through the meadows ; but, when
he came to London, he resolutely cast all that
aside, as a man born to a fine estate and
brought suddenly to beggary is wise to try to
forget the past and do the best possible for
the future.

For years Jack had wilfully ignored all
causes of anxiety ; but from the time he was
advanced to the post of manager, something

more than a vague sense of uneasiness began
to oppress him. Hitherto he had never
known any want of money; debts incurred
without the wherewithal to discharge them
were things unheard of in Fowkes' Buildings.
Years previously he had insured his life for
a moderate amount; but circumstances were
changed since then. His responsibilities had
increased; his wife's views grown larger;
what would once have seemed a decent
provision for a rainy day now could be
regarded but as a drop in the ocean of the
family's increased expenditure.

Mr. Jeffley could close his eyes to facts no
longer. Let his salary be as good as Messrs.
Deedes liked to make it, a use could somehow
be found for the whole stipend.

What Frank Scott said was too true. He
had not saved a shilling—no, not a penny
likely to benefit himself, supposing he lived
to be an old man and grow past his work;
the insurances did not amount to much, and,
if he increased them, he was not so young as
he had been, and the premiums would tot up
to something considerable. He ought not to

let this great windfall—this gift straight from
Heaven, as it seemed to him—be frittered
away, and yet it was hard at that time of his
married life to begin to keep money from
his wife. Jack did not know what to do.
He turned and twisted matters over in his
mind, and was still so turning and twisting
them when he fell ill and made quite sure his
last hour had come.

That fifteen hundred pounds lay heavy on
his soul. He had made no arrangement
concerning it, not even mentioned the legacy
to his wife. In the dead of night he lay and
thought about his widow and his children,
remembered the precise tone in which Frank
Scott had uttered his warning, and lamented
he had not put on his considering-cap while
his head was still clear enough to consider
anything. If he had seen any good which
making a will could do, he would even at the
eleventh hour have sent for a lawyer ; but it
was difficult to make up his mind how it
would be best to parcel the money out.
Curiously enough, it was when he seemed
physically at his weakest that his brain began

to clear. Lying free from pain, but in a state of absolute exhaustion, he saw no longer as through a mist dimly, but clearly what he considered the best and only road to take.

" I'll settle the matter the first day I can get out," he decided ; and, having so settled it, he waited with patience in the twilight, waiting till his wife should have finished her sleep, and dressed, and be in a condition inwardly and outwardly to listen to what he had to say.

It was past five o'clock before Mrs. Jeffley, dressed in her second-best silk dress, rustled down the staircase. The gas had long been lighted all over the house, save in his own especial room—that room in which, though Jack did not know it, his wife had beheld a vision which over and over again softened and changed her manner in a way which seemed to everyone, Mrs. Childs alone excepted, unaccountable.

But all that was passing now. In precise proportion to the amount of wine, beef-tea, jelly, and beaten-up eggs her husband swallowed, Mrs. Jeffley's heart hardened.

She was anxious about the patient no longer. He had been able to go into the City; he talked of getting round to the office. She felt inclined to resent the extent to which her feelings had been lacerated, and occasionally she said very sharp things indeed to Jack. The weather further was wretched, and some of her inmates had been giving her trouble— altogether, Mrs. Jeffley was not in the best of tempers on that evening when she bustled downstairs, and, flinging wide the parlour-door, let in a flood of light, against which her husband involuntarily closed his tired eyes.

" What—all in the dark ?" she cried. " I am sure that is not the way to get well ; moping and thinking is the worst thing in the world for anyone ;" and, suiting her practice to her precept, she turned the gas full on and lit all three burners.

" Come, that's better," she remarked. " You feel stronger, don't you ? Been asleep ?"

" No," answered Jack.

" Oh! but I am sure you must have been. I was so tired, the minute I lay down I went off; but then, of course, it is different with me. I have never sat down since breakfast, except when I tried to swallow a mouthful of dinner."

"Can't you sit down now?" asked her husband.

"At this time of the evening! Shows how much you know about all I have to do."

"But I want to speak to you."

"Speak then. What is hindering you?"

"I wish you would shut the door."

"Dear me! There—will that content you? Now what is this great mystery?"

"It is no great mystery—it relates to money."

"Money!" she repeated sharply. "You have not got into any money trouble, I hope?"

"No. Do sit down, Maria—I want to talk to you seriously. You have no idea how it worries me to see you standing and fidgeting, as if you wanted every instant to go."

"Well, I do want to go. However! if I must stop and listen to you, I suppose I must. Make haste though—everything is behind to-night, as it always is if I take a quarter of an hour's rest."

" I will make as much haste as I can. I have been very very ill, you know."

" If I don't know, it is not because you have not told me so often enough. Whether you have been very ill or not, however, you are getting well now."

" That is as it may be," said Jack.

" That is as it is," returned Mrs. Jeffley, with great decision.

" Well—well—let that pass. If I get well now, I may not be so lucky the next time."

" Bless me! if you are not enough to provoke a saint. What would hinder you getting well fifty times if you were fifty times ill?—which I hope with all my heart and soul you won't be! Once has been quite enough. If you couldn't get well, I'd like to know who ought: good food—a warm house—the best of nursing—the doctor to see you not less than twice a day! Why, if you had been a king you couldn't have had more care taken of you!"

" I don't deny that; but," Jack hurried on

(seeing a look in his wife's face which meant
"because you can't"), "what I wanted to say
was, when once a man gets his marching
order for another world, the best of good care
can't hinder him."

"Can't it?" said Mrs. Jeffley drily.

"And when I was at my worst, I felt just
as a soldier might the night before a battle,
while he lies thinking of his wife and
children."

"The doctor would not like your talking in
this sort of way," observed his wife. "I
know I don't; and you're keeping me from
what I ought to be doing."

"The doctor said if I had anything weighing
on me I ought to get it off my mind as soon
as I could," answered Jack.

"And have you anything weighing on
you?"

"Yes."

"Then why don't you do what the doctor
tells you?"

"I will, if you will only hear what it is."

"Oh! I'll listen fast enough, only do not
keep me here all night."

"I have been very anxious about you and the children."

"You told me that before."

"Yes; and I must tell you again, because that is the burden of the whole trouble. Of course I should like to live as well as anybody else, still, if it is God's will I should die——"

"You are not going to die," declared Mrs. Jeffley, as if she were the Almighty.

"Well, anyhow, whether I die or live I want to put affairs as straight for you as I can, and I began to do so to-day."

"What have you been doing? Tiring yourself, for one thing, I see. I only hope you have not been catching a fresh cold," which remark was flung at Jack as though he had been out fishing for quinsy.

"I have been transferring some stock to your name."

"Stock!" repeated his wife. "In the name of patience what sort of stock?"

"Consols—Three per Cents—Government Securities. Fact is, Polly," proceeded Mr. Jeffley, taking a leap at this point over an extremely stiff hedge and ditch—a rasper indeed—"my godmother has died and left me some money."

"Left you some money!" repeated Mrs. Jeffley. She had been the proud possessor of two godmothers, and yet neither had thought of leaving *her* any money.

"Yes; and what I thought, d'ye see, dear, was this—supposing I die without a will!"

"But you are not going to die," repeated the lady with even greater decision than before.

"We must all die," said Jack mournfully. Spite of the boarding-house and his wife's "little hastinesses," as he mentally termed her fits of ill-temper, and Mr. Katzen, he did think this world a very pleasant one, and would have liked to stop in it for a very long time.

"I am not so sure of that," answered Mrs. Jeffley, who at times really did seem to consider herself omnipotent.

"At any rate, many people do die," hazarded her husband, "and likely some day I may be one of the lot. For this reason I must tell you how it would be if before I went I made no will—one-third the law would give to you, and the remainder would be divided equally among the children."

"I know that."

"Well, surely you could do better for the young ones, if your hands were not tied. I don't hold, myself, with leaving money to boys and girls that they are entitled to without 'thank you' or 'by your leave' from their parents."

"It is not over-probable *your* boys and girls will inherit enough from you to trouble them," said Mrs. Jeffley contemptuously.

"Perhaps you are right, but still, what there is I'd like to know was in your hands. I can just as well say to you all I should put in a will if I made one. I have put the whole of this legacy in Consols in your name —you will have the papers in a few days. It is yours absolutely, mind. If I live I shall never want it from you again; the only thing is, I should like you to make me two promises."

"What promises?" asked Mrs. Jeffley.

"One, that you won't use it in this boarding-house business; and the other, that if you marry again, you will secure the money to our children."

"You may be very sure I shall never marry again."

She did not remark aloud, "I have found once too often;" but Jack, reading the addition plainly as though it had been printed on her face, wisely abstained from further discussion on that point.

"I am sure you will do what I ask," he said.

"Oh! I'll do what you ask," she agreed ungraciously. "You have never asked me much I have not been only too willing to grant, though what can be your hatred to a business which has kept us all in comfort and respectability baffles me."

"That has nothing to do with the present matter. All I want is for this money, which has fallen in a manner from the clouds, to be kept by itself, always available for you and the children. I'd like the interest to accumulate, if you find no immediate need for it."

"I dare say the interest won't signify much

one way or other," said Mrs. Jeffley disparag-
ingly.

" I do not know exactly what it will come
to. Nearly fifty pounds a year, I suppose."

" *Nearly what ?*"

" Say five-and-forty—it will be that, at any
rate."

" Why, how much has been left you ?"

" Fifteen hundred pounds !"

Mrs. Jeffley looked at her husband in
blank amazement. If he had been trying
with the greatest art to lead up to a telling
situation, he could scarcely have succeeded
better.

" Fifteen hundred !" she repeated. " Well,
I never !"

" If it had only been a trifle, I shouldn't
have troubled about it," Mr. Jeffley said simply
—" I'd have put it into your hand straight
away, and asked you to buy what you fancied
for yourself and the children ; but——"

Jack paused. He was still low and weak,
and even had he felt in strong health, he
would have hesitated how to word what he
still wished to add.

Mrs. Jeffley did not make any remark. For once speech failed her—for once the man's childlike confidence and faithful love touched her soul without stirring her anger.

Fifteen hundred pounds just handed over with less fuss than many a husband would have made about doling out a sovereign. And Jack did look ill and changed. In the glare of the gaslight, and with the leaping flame, into which she had stirred the blazing coals, falling at cross angles upon his face, she could see how thin he was—how haggard —how unlike the strong, healthy, burly Jack it once seemed as though sickness could never touch, and who, in his wife's eyes, could do no single thing that was right.

Involuntarily almost, she put up her hand between herself and the fire, which for a moment seemed to flicker and waver as though seen through water. Still she did not speak, and, emboldened perhaps by her unwonted silence, Jack took courage, and went on :

" I scarcely know how to put it without seeming foolish, but I could not be off thinking that this money ought to be kept safe for a rainy day. Supposing I were disabled, or you laid up, where would we all be if we had nothing saved ?"

" You reckon the goodwill of such a house as this nothing, I suppose ?" interrupted Mrs. Jeffley, all the more angrily because she had felt so "soft and foolish for a minute." " We'd have been a nice set of paupers on the face of the earth all these years if it hadn't been for this house, I can tell you !"

" I don't quite go with you there," said Jack. " We need not have been paupers, anyhow ; and though we have had plenty of food, we have had very little good of our home. For my own part, if I could choose, I would rather have a crust and a place, no matter how small, all to ourselves, than live on the best, and see you at the beck and call of every disreputable old sailor who can find money enough to pay for his quarters."

" Yes, I think I see you sitting down to a crust and saying grace over it," said Mrs. Jeffley, in high dudgeon ; " and as for my boarders, I would have you know I allow no one disreputable inside my doors. If you had done as much for your family as I have, we should be very differently situated from what we are—very differently indeed!"

"Somehow," said Jack, "I am always wrong. Well, it may be I am as poor a fellow as you think, still, as men go, I haven't made you a bad husband. You might have got somebody richer, cleverer, handsomer, but you could never have found mortal could love you better. And you liked me once, Maria, you did! What has come between us God only knows! I am sure I don't. I wish I did. I wish I could tell how to set matters right. But they will never come right now— never!" and, turning his face from the light, he burst into a passion of tears.

"Jack—Jack!" cried his wife, frightened by this unprecedented demonstration, "don't do that! You'll make yourself ill again— you'll throw yourself back! Jack, do try— there's a dear!" and she laid a hand on his shoulder and stooped over him, while the man, utterly weak and broken, sobbed on.

"What will the doctor say?" exclaimed Mrs. Jeffley, fairly in despair. "What can I do ? Jack—Jack, for my sake, for the children's sake——"

He had her hand now, and was kissing it passionately. The old days of courtship seemed to have come back again, only with the love which once had been sweet and silly intensified into tragedy. "Oh, my wife," he moaned—"oh, my wife !"

The words seemed wrung from him in very anguish.

"What is it, Jack?" she asked, stooping over him very low, stooping till the face he still thought beautiful touched his hair.

For answer, he released her hand, and tried feebly to pass his arm round her neck.

"H—sh!" said Mrs. Jeffley. "There is some one at the door."

Jack's arm dropped as if stricken. Mrs. Jeffley raised her head and cried, "Come in !"

"If you please, 'm," explained the last new servant, "Mr. Katzen is back, and Miss Weir would like to see you if convenient."

CHAPTER X.

THE OLD, OLD STORY.

HEN Mrs. Jeffley left her husband, which she did immediately, only pausing to turn down the gas, and put a newspaper over the back of a chair she placed between him and the fire (unwonted attentions Jack, even though he did not look up, noticed and felt keenly)—she passed out into the hall, where she found Miss Weir standing on a mat at one side, and Mr. Katzen leaning up against the wall on the other side. They were within easy speaking distance, a distance of not more than three feet dividing them, and appeared to be utilizing their opportunity.

"I am glad to see you both," said Mrs.

Jeffley, extending a friendly hand to each—
"Welcome home, Mr. Katzen. As for Miss
Weir, she knows she is always welcome."

"How is Mr. Jeffley?" asked Abigail.

"A little tired this evening—he has been
out to-day, but on the whole better—yes,
better certainly. Run upstairs and take off
your bonnet, and then we will all have a cup
of tea together. A sight of you will cheer
my husband up."

"Don't believe her, Abigail," interrupted
the Consul. "Mr. Jeffley wants no one—
can want no one to cheer him up but his own
wife. You had better accept my invitation,
and enjoy a cup of tea with me *tête-à-tête*.
You shall see what a lot of nice things I
have in my bag for good little girls."

"When you find the good little girls, it
will be time enough for you to exhibit your
treasures," replied Miss Weir.

"But where," asked Mr. Katzen, "could I
find so good a little girl as you?"

"Good little girls are seen, not heard,"
returned Abigail, "but wherever I am seen, I
am heard."

" That is so, my dear, and it is your saucy tongue which adds such a delight to life when one is in your company."

Mrs. Jeffley listened with some displeasure. This was a sort of thing she dimly felt to be improper, unless she were chief actress in the drama. Her idea of a good piece was that it should be all Mrs. Jeffley—and behold here was one put on the boards of her own house, in which no real part seemed assigned her, scarcely even that of spectator.

This jesting pair—were they really only jesting ?—could do with her ; but not all the lady's egotism was able to blind her to the fact that they could do just as well without her.

An uneasy feeling crept over her, the same sort of chill which might assail a somewhat *passée* prima donna if she were suddenly to be transported from a loyal audience to some dreadful music-hall, where no one knew her, and the pet of the period was delighting her especial admirers with an archly comic song.

Mrs. Jeffley had but just stepped off the boards of her own theatre, where half unconsciously she played the part of heroine, in what would have been described on huge posters as a thrilling domestic drama, and behold this was the nice little after-piece on which it seemed to be supposed she could look with approval.

"I did not think it was quite right," she said afterwards when referring to the matter; "at any rate, I knew I could not have such goings on just inside my front door."

"Run upstairs, Miss Weir," she repeated, with an effort to seem genial which was creditable under the circumstances; "take no notice of his folly. I will be after you in a moment."

"Thank you greatly," answered Abby, "but I cannot stop—I cannot indeed. I only wanted to explain to you that I have enough material left to make one smaller frock. Shall I use it up, or would you rather keep the piece in case of accidents?"

"She would rather keep the piece, of course," interrupted Mr. Katzen. "Don't you know how fond Mrs. Jeffley is of planning, and patching, and cheeseparing?

No liberality about her—likes to see the children's clothes well darned: that sort of thing."

"If I had been fonder of 'that sort of thing,' perhaps I might be better off now," said Mrs. Jeffley tartly. "However, it is never too late to mend. Make up the little frock by all means, Miss Weir, only do not stand there. If you would rather not go upstairs, have tea in your bonnet. There is no one in the parlour but Mr. Jeffley; tea will be ready in five minutes."

"I must not wait, thank you—I would rather not indeed," answered Abigail. "I will say good-evening now, please."

"Don't hinder her," interposed Mr. Katzen, as Mrs. Jeffley was about recommencing her hospitable entreaties. "She has to be back in time to see that the kettle is boiling when the old gentleman comes home."

"What old gentleman?" asked the girl.

'The young gentleman then," laughed Mr. Katzen.

"If you mean Mr. Brisco," said Abigail,

"it so happens that he will not be home to-night."

"Ho! ho!" exclaimed the Consul, "what, are you all alone in the old house, dear Abby?"

"No, Mr. Katzen. I am not all alone in the old house. I am not so fond of being alone in it as I was once. Miss Greaves is stopping with me."

"Miss Greaves cannot be much of a companion—I shall come round presently to cheer you up a little."

"If you do—you will not get in."

"That is right—you keep him at a distance," put in Mrs. Jeffley.

"Ah! I have never yet given up my latch-key," said Mr. Katzen.

"Your latch-key won't take down the chain," retorted Abigail. "I really must go now, Mrs. Jeffley. Good-evening.—Good-evening, Mr. Katzen."

"Wait but one moment," entreated that gentleman, "and I will walk round with you. I only go to get a muffler—the wind has changed, and my throat feels the London damp."

Abigail did not answer. She stood watching him while he ran upstairs, then, saying to Mrs. Jeffley, " I shan't wait," she departed.

Before she could have reached the bottom of the court Mr. Katzen was in the hall again.

" Where is she ?" he asked.

" Gone," answered Mrs. Jeffley, with a spiteful smile. " She would not wait, and quite right too."

Mr. Katzen did not stop to hear the end of the sentence. In a moment he was out of Fowkes' Buildings and hurrying along Great Tower Street. " The little imp," he muttered—" the cunning little minx—how fast she must have gone! Never mind, I shall catch her yet."

But, as it happened, he did not catch her— even in Love Lane. The old house was in utter darkness. It being Saturday, the offices had long been deserted, and not a ray of light gleamed from any window. He stood on the top of the high flight of steps and knocked without eliciting any answer—then he tried his key, but the catch was up ; again he knocked—again and again he rang—till it seemed as if every room in the house echoed the sound.

Angry and baffled, he at length retraced his way to Fowkes' Buildings. "Ah! my dear," he thought, "you have your way now ; when it is my turn, you shall see. No doubt, hidden behind the door, you were laughing in your sleeve at my discomfiture. It is all very well for a while—but you may go too far."

Had he known that Abigail, instead of being hidden behind the door, was not even in the house, he would have felt more confident even than he did that her conduct was not at all well, and that she was going very far indeed. It never occurred to him she could have turned in any other direction than back to her form ; yet, in truth, the moment she found herself in Great Tower Street, she scudded off in the direction of Trinity Square as fast as her active young legs could carry her.

At the back of All Hallows she dodged up

a paved passage from whence, threading her way through Seething Lane and Muscovy Court, she at length, sometimes running, sometimes walking, arrived by no short cut in Swan Street; keeping the dark side of the thoroughfare, she hurried on till, sharply turning the corner of Great Prescot Street, she ran against a man coming from the opposite direction.

"Take care!" he exclaimed. "I hope you have not hurt yourself. *Why, Abby*——"

"Oh, Frank," she said, and then stood silent, trembling a little and waiting to recover her breath.

"What is the matter?" he asked. "Why are you so late, and why were you racing at such a speed?"

"I was detained at Mrs. Jeffley's," she answered, panting; "and I thought you would be waiting, and——"

"Let us walk on slowly," he suggested. "Why did you go to Mrs. Jeffley's?"

"I wanted to speak to her—and I could not. I had to come away—Mr. Katzen was there."

" He is back, is he ?—and he accompanied you on your road, I suppose ?"

" No ; he said he would go back to Love Lane with me ; but I managed to slip off without him."

" You were afraid, however, he might be following you, I suppose ?"

" Yes, I frightened myself—but I am not frightened now," she added, " I do not care. As I came along I made up my mind— quite."

" Made up your mind on what subject ?"

" That I would meet you no more in this way, Frank."

" Never again ?"

" Never again at all. If you really cared for me you would not ask me to do it. It is not right, and what is not right——"

" Must be wrong," finished the young man. " Did you find all this out since you left Fowkes' Buildings ?"

" I found it out long ago," she answered ; " but I was a coward, I would not confess the truth even to myself. I said, ' Frank must know best. He would not ask me to meet him in this way unless he had some good reason;' but to-night I see the whole thing differently. As I came along I felt so lonely, so desolate, so deceitful."

" Have you been deceiving me ?" he asked.

" No, not you; there is nothing about myself I have not told you, except——"

" That you care for me no longer."

She shook her head. " I do care for you just the same as ever ; but I can't go on with this secrecy. It is treacherous. What would Mr. Brisco think of me if he knew ?"

" Perhaps he would not take the matter so very much to heart after all."

" He might not take it to heart—there is no one in the wide world likely to take to heart what I do or leave undone—but he would despise me—and quite right too. I ought not to have been sly and underhand. And, oh, Frank! you should not have asked me to be false. If I were your sister, and you knew she was meeting a man as I have been meeting you, what should you say to her and him ?"

" I cannot tell."

" Yes, you can tell ; you would say of them both just what Mrs. Jeffley and Mr. Katzen would say of us if they suspected anything of the sort. There was a time when I thought there could be no harm in it all, but I know better now."

He drew a long breath. " Perhaps you are wise," he answered. " Indeed, I am sure you are wise to have nothing more to do with such an unfortunate devil as I am."

" Unfortunate !" she repeated. " Now you have got this wonderful situation, and things are going so smoothly with you ! What can you mean ?"

" That I am unfortunate," he said doggedly. " My whole life long, if a piece of what I believed to be good luck came in my way, it was always sure to be followed by some greater stroke of evil."

" What has happened to you now ?" she asked.

" I cannot tell you, Abby, more than this. You know I hoped when I got this berth to be able very shortly to make a clean breast to Mr. Brisco and ask him for you."

" Yes—I—know," she said faintly.

" Well, I can't do that now. I do not know when I shall stand in a position to justify the hope that he will listen to me."

" Oh !" It was the only word Abby could speak, the mean, dirty street seemed to be whirling round and round with her, and her heart beat quicker and more loudly than it had done even when with twinkling feet she was flying from Mr. Katzen's fancied pursuit.

" You see now," went on Frank, " why I said you were wise."

" I am trying to understand," she answered, in a low, strained voice. " I know what I meant; I want now to know what you mean."

" You meant you were tired of our clandestine courtship ; what I mean is, that I see no likelihood of being able to go with you hand-in-hand to Mr. Brisco and make a full and free confession of the great sin we have committed in caring for one another."

" You are really serious !"

" Serious ! Is it likely I should joke about losing you ? Does a man joke when he feels

he is about to have the one thing he values
wrested from him ?"

" But, Frank, why should you lose me ?"

" You yourself have said——"

They walked on a little farther in utter
silence ; then she stopped.

" I think I had better go home now," she
remarked, putting out her hand, which had
suddenly grown cold as ice.

He did not answer " No" or " Yes," he
only took her hand and held it fast. The
girl did not try to extricate it ; she stood
like one numbed. She had not expected
perhaps to be taken so strictly at her word.
Explanations, remonstrances, reproaches, entreaties—all sours and sweets, all the fennel
and honey which we are taught in books is
the food of love—she was prepared to meet ;
but this awful acquiescence—this unquestion-
ing acceptance of her expressed decision—
pierced her heart.

Yet had she known—it is just thus that
lovers mostly part in real life.

Without thought they break the mirror in
which they have so often fondly contemplated

the fair future they trust to walk through side
by side for life, and the shattered atoms lie
strewed around them before they realize they
have done what never can be undone—
destroyed something very beautiful it is
beyond their power to restore.

Dimly Abigail began to comprehend something of all this—of how lives are wrecked,
and lovers parted, and human ships, freighted
with rich and goodly cargoes, lost.

She knew great sorrows came to some
people, but it had never occurred to her till
then that such cruel suffering could come to
her.

What had she done—oh, what had she
done, unconsciously, her heart was already
asking, that it should thus be rent? In its
wild fright and anguish it was beating against
the iron bars of a cage made by its own free
will. To be taken at her word thus—well, if
he could part with her, best so—best by far.
After a little she would argue it all out quietly
by herself; but just then she felt dulled and
chill. A noise inaudible to the outer world,
but maddening to her, was going on in her

brain. Fifty hammers might have been beating upon it and confused her less.

"Come on with me a little farther," he said at last ; " it cannot signify now."

" No," she agreed mechanically.

No indeed, it did not signify—not at all— if Mr. Brisco, and Mr. Katzen, and Mrs. Jeffley, and the inhabitants of the three parishes in which she might be said to live, had all appeared before her at that moment ; she would not have cared. The greater includes the less ; in the broad sea of trouble now sweeping over the sweet promise of her love, what signified such wretched trifles as man's opinion, and woman's doubts ?

She would never walk beside him any more—that was how her thought ran—and oh ! how sweet their walks had been, haloed with that light which never yet was seen on land or sea—that light which changed the narrow City lanes into pleached alleys, roofed with greenery, bordered with flowers, turfed with moss and thyme !

They had skirted Goodman's Fields, where once Stow was wont to repair for milk from the farm, now an aggregation of closely packed houses, and were in Leman Street.

To Abigail all ways seemed alike. When sentence has been delivered, it matters little which route is taken to the scaffold.

Still Frank did not speak. In silence he turned into a little graveyard which might have been out of the world for all signs of life it contained.

The quiet dead who lay there, long buried, long forgotten, made no stir, no moan. Happy dead, thought Abigail—who could suffer and fret no more ; man might not hurt, or love touch them. They walked to the end of the court, then Frank suddenly stopped.

" Abigail," he said hoarsely, and then, before she could answer him, he threw his arms round the girl and strained her to his heart.

" I *can't* give you up, my darling," he murmured, passionately kissing her over and over again.

It was the first time he had so held—the first time he had ever kissed her. " My love —my dear—my own," and then, half ashamed and repenting of his vehemence, he would have released her, but she nestled her face against his shoulder, while her whole frame was shaken with sobs.

"Forgive me," he whispered, "I could not help it. Oh! sweet, I might give up my life, but not you. Look at me, you are not angry? You know, Abigail, I would not vex you for the world."

She did not say a word, yet she gave him the sweetest, most natural answer possible, by lifting her face to his bent down over hers, and letting her lips just touch his own.

Poor lonely dead! long buried, long forgotten; who could never again feel the rapture which filled those two young hearts to overflowing—who had done with the sunshine as with the sorrow, for whom, if there were no more earthly mourning, there could be no more earthly joy.

Wearily and with leaden feet she had traversed those streets through which they returned slowly, in order to lengthen that delicious hour of reconciliation.

"What was it which came between us?" Abigail at last asked wonderingly.

37—2

"Why trouble ourselves about that?" he answered. "Nothing shall ever come between us again."

So they walked on, talking folly as lovers do, repeating the old, old story—old as the world, new as to-day—ringing every possible change on that sweet peal of bells which pours forth such music on the lightest touch of inexperienced hands.

"Frank," said the girl at last, "I want to tell you something that I have kept back from you. Something that I did once."

"Something very bad?" he asked tenderly, yet with a sinking heart.

"I am afraid, very bad."

"When did you commit this great sin?" He tried to put the question easily, even airily, but the attempt proved a conspicuous failure.

She averted her head a little. "I was a child—I had not been long in the old house——"

"I want to hear nothing about it, then," he interrupted in a tone of glad relief. "For God's sake, Abby, bury that wretched past, and don't put up even a foot-stone to its memory. Why should you make yourself miserable by talking about that terrible time ? I am steadfastly determined you shall not talk, to me at any rate, about it."

She sighed softly while she murmured, " Very well." What would Mr. Katzen have said to this obedient little maiden ? Surely he must have exclaimed, " Here is a change-ling ; this can't be Abigail !"

" Sometimes I wish," she began, and then paused, hesitating.

" What do you sometimes wish ?"

" That you would talk to *me* about *your-self.*"

" It seems to me I have few other topics of conversation," he observed evasively.

" Ah ! I do not mean about yourself latterly," she explained. " I should like to know all that has happened to you since the beginning. What is the first thing you remember ?"

" Meeting Abigail Weir," he replied. " I date from that minute. I want to remember no other event in my life. I only began to live then. I had suffered before ; but that day the blessed light dawned upon me existence was worth having——"

" But Frank——"

" My dearest, listen to me. I have not always been a 'good boy.' I have been a bad boy, on the contrary, and if it had not chanced that I was pulled up in time, you and I should never have known each other. I don't mean," he added, seeing the pained and startled look in the girl's face, "that I have committed any great crime—but I did things I ought not to have done, and I left undone those which I ought to have done. I won't go on with my profitless confession. Let us agree to abandon retrospect——"

" Very well," she said again, but she said the words sorrowfully.

" Does it seem hard to you?" he asked with a quick remorse. " Well, then, I promise that some day you shall know all. If I can remember even how many apples I stole when a schoolboy, you shall have a full list. Are you satisfied now ?"

" Never tell me anything if it hurts you," she answered softly. They threaded the courts that lie so close together near the Trinity House, sauntering through them over and over again. Then they walked many times around the square so called. It seemed as though they could not bear to part. They talked scarcely at all; their love had entered upon another stage. It was enough for them to be together; speech was unnecessary, speech would have been poor indeed to express what two so fond, so foolish, felt. A lonely young man, solitary in a great city; as lonely a young girl, earning a poor living by her own exertions, dependent upon a stranger for the shelter she called home. Adam and Eve wandering among the fair flowers of a sinless Eden were not more solitary than this pair, desolate, save for each other, in the wilderness of wicked London.

"I must be going, Frank," said Abigail at last. "Miss Greaves will be wondering where I can have got to."

He did not immediately reply. Instead, he looked at the girl wistfully.

"So we are to meet no more?" he said at last.

"You won't ask me," she answered.

" No, I won't ask you ;" and they drew a little nearer to Thames Street.

"I am afraid ours will have to be a long engagement," he resumed, after a pause.

" I do not mind how long," she said. " But perhaps, after a time, you will let me tell Mr. Brisco ?"

" Well—no. I think matters must wait, so far as he is concerned."

" Do you know, Frank, I cannot help fancying you are wrong ? I am sure Mr. Brisco would not object to you in the least— why should he ? What I fear he never could forgive would be our deception ; I am obliged to call it deception, though we never meant to deceive him."

" *I* did," corrected the young man.

" Well, at all events, do not let us deceive him any longer. From the beginning, the one thing he impressed upon me was the necessity of telling the truth."

" Oh ! it was, was it ?"

" Yes ; and that is the reason I do so dread his finding out anything about this, except from ourselves. He might forgive me now if

I explained how it all came about ; but he would never speak to me again, I truly believe, if he heard about you from any one else. I know him thoroughly, Frank—indeed I do !"

" You know nothing about Mr. Brisco," said the young man, a little roughly.

" If I do not know him, who should ?" she asked.

" That is a question I really cannot answer," replied Mr. Frank ; " but I feel confident you have as little real acquaintance with his character as you had, poor child, the first night he found you starved and sick, lying like a hunted animal in the old house."

Abigail bit her lip. There was something in her lover's tone which hurt her ; there had often been something in it lately, when speaking of Mr. Brisco, she failed to understand.

" Whether I understand him or not," she answered a little hotly, " I know he has been kind to me. I owe him a debt of gratitude I can never repay, and it seems to me a poor return to make for all his goodness to keep such a secret from him."

The young fellow smiled a little sadly.

"Nothing was ever to come between us again," he quoted; "nothing shall ever come between us again. If you feel that it would be best for me to speak to Mr. Brisco at once, I will do so the moment he returns. I have my own opinion on the subject, but let that pass. I will do just what you please."

"No, no!" she answered eagerly; "it must be as you please. The only thing which perplexes me is that a short time ago you were anxious to enter into your new occupation, so as to tell Mr. Brisco—about—me, and now——"

"All that is changed, you mean, I suppose?" he said, as she hesitated.

"Yes, you have been vexed or discouraged in some way. Are you not doing so well as you expected?"

"Quite as well; but I know now how poor I am really, spite of this promotion—the sort of reception I should meet with if I asked Mr. Brisco for you."

"But, Frank, you are rich in comparison with us."

"Are you sure of that?"

" Certain ! Who could be poorer than we are ?"

" Are you sure Mr. Brisco *is* so badly off ?"

" Of course I am. I do not see how he could well be worse off."

" And if I told you that he might live differently, that he possesses the means to live differently, you would not believe me ?"

" I should believe you believed what you said ; but that would not make the statement true."

" Have you never heard or read of such a thing as a man grudging himself the common necessaries of existence, even though worth thousands."

" Of course ; but not such a man as Mr. Brisco. He is no miser."

" How do you know ?"

" Misers hide things. They are like magpies ; they hide for concealment's sake. They pick up pieces of iron, and store away old bones, and put away money in all sorts of odd places."

" Yes ?"

" And Mr. Brisco hides away nothing.

He has only one little drawer which he keeps locked, and there is nothing in it but papers. I have seen him open it often. There are those old trunks I told you about ; anyone could look over every article they contain. Some person has been hoaxing you, Frank."

" Well, we shall see. But suppose a day should come when you found Mr. Brisco had not been so poor, after all—that during the time he was living meanly and meagrely himself, and only giving you enough food to keep body and soul together, he could have afforded a decent expenditure—what would your feelings be towards him then ?"

" It is an impossible case," answered Abigail ; " but, if it were possible, I might feel sorry, but I could not feel angry. Why do you say such hard, bitter things to-night ; why are you trying to harden my heart against a man who has never done evil to me ? Supposing even he were rich, had I a right to his money ? Am I his kith or kin that I should say, 'You did not give me enough'—I, with whom he shared his store—I, who was thankful to crawl into

his house out of the icy cold and cruel
damp ?"

" God bless you, Abby !" cried the young
man, as she paused, breathless and excited.
" You are indeed grateful for small mer-
cies."

" Do you call them small ? I look back
and feel as if I could not be grateful enough.
Frank, it is not kind of you ; it is not right.
If I could only make you see Mr. Brisco as I
see him—only make you know him as I know
him !"

" You would be able to perform a miracle,"
interrupted Frank ; " but I won't vex you
any more about him, though I may tell you I
would give a great deal to be able to think of
your benefactor as you do."

" Ah ! then it will all come right some day.
Do not listen to what any evil-disposed
person may have to say. I think I know
where you got this absurd notion—at the
Jeffleys', was it not ? Very likely Mrs.
Childs has originated some fancy of the sort.
Say it was Mrs. Childs, Frank, do !"

" Well, perhaps Mrs. Childs may have had

some share in originating the idea," he answered slowly.

" I thought it was the Childs' sign-manual and superscription. Good-night—good-bye. Don't think any more evil of Mr. Brisco ;" and, without giving him time to answer, she flitted rapidly away.

Walking swiftly, she turned from Lower Thames Street into the covered, paved, and vile-smelling alley which leads to the back entrance of Sir Christopher's old house. Arrived there, she did not trip up the steps and demand ingress at the door where Mr. Katzen had sought admission in vain. Another lock yielded quite easily to her key, and by the kitchen staircase she made her way into the hall.

In the panelled dining-room, beside an almost expiring fire, Miss Greaves sat fast asleep. Her candle was burning down into the socket ; her book had fallen on the floor ; her mouth was open, and her cap awry.

" Bless me !" she exclaimed, starting as Abigail crossed the room. " I think I must have dropped off for a moment."

CHAPTER XI.

THE NEW LOAN.

T was midsummer. The year's golden prime had come. In London the heat could only be described as suffocating ; not a breath of air seemed to temper the oven-like atmosphere.

Into Fowkes' Buildings, as though it were some dim grot, Mrs. Jeffley's mates and captains turned gratefully, taking off their hats and mopping their foreheads with gorgeous pocket-handkerchiefs, while they walked leisurely up the court. But even in that retreat, where the sun's rays scarcely ever penetrated, the temperature was extraordinarily high. Mrs. Jeffley declared she felt at her wits' end in the way of catering.

"Butchers' meat," she said, "will scarcely keep till we can get it down before the fire ; and as for bacon, there is not a gammon rasher to be had in the City for love or money ; and my people will eat nothing else."

But for strong drinks, indeed, poor Mrs. Jeffley's position would have been pitiable. To cool themselves her gentlemen imbibed fiery liquors, diluted with as little water as was practicable ; indeed, an opinion prevailed among all the inmates of her house that water was well-nigh as dangerous as poison, and required to be used with like caution. At various times of the day and night, re-marks were thrown out as to the known bad character of water, and the ill-effects certain to ensue from trifling with it. This was the reason why Captain Hassell and others of the same stamp were always about that period in a state of torrid heat.

"If you struck a match near one of them," observed Mr. Katzen to Frank Scott, "he'd light like gunpowder."

It was weather in which the German revelled. Trade chanced to be good—ice plentiful, claret-cup procurable at every tavern. What could a man—and a foreigner—want more ?

He was doing well at last. The tide had turned—that tide which he once began to think meant to go on ebbing for ever—and the waves of Fortune were flowing surely, though in his impatience he sometimes imagined slowly, to the bare shore on which he had stood for so long, contemplating a sad expanse of barren sand.

Now he could afford to be insolent, or indifferent, or patronising, just as the mood took him, to those who had once mocked his ill-success and underrated his powers of recuperation. No sneaking through back streets now ; no sudden disappearance into the shade of friendly courts and gloom of mysterious alleys ; no effort to escape inopportune meetings with too familiar duns ; no painful smiles or hastily assumed cheerfulness of manner. Just then Mr. Katzen felt he could almost have turned his heart inside out for general inspection.

For once, it was so free from guile, so

clear of reproach, so full of the milk of human kindness, so honest, so clean.

The sensation must have been novel. In all his life, indeed, the Consul had never known his body inhabited by a like spirit, and occasionally he found the new tenant strange to the extent of being disagreeable.

But he made the most out of his unwonted position. Where (in the City) men do congregate, Mr. Katzen was generally to be found. About The Exchange and Bartholomew Lane and Throgmorton Street, the Consul for New Andalusia flitted like a bat. Persons who had business in Cornhill and Lombard Street met him in those thoroughfares; they saw him conversing with men who were known to take their thousands and tens of thousands with less fuss than a beggar makes about looking at the reverse side of a penny; old creditors, who had lost money by Mr. Katzen in former days, and shown him the cold shoulder ever since, began to nod and smile, and make friendly advances; some even from afar shaking those two fingers at him which in the City constitute an outward and visible sign of close acquaintance. The manager of the bank where once his modest balance was scanned scornfully, and clerks smiled covertly to each other as they " referred back " when a cheque of the Consul's was presented across the counter, began to say,—" How de do, Mr. Katzen ?" if he chanced to espy the little foreigner when passing through to his especial sanctum after luncheon.

As marriage is popularly supposed to make honest women of women who stand in great need of such rehabilitation, in like manner, money reputation, which in the City so often supplies the place of virtue, was, in Mr. Katzen's case, about to be taken as twenty shillings in the pound in settlement of all the Consul's former moral bankruptcies.

That he would never pay any old debt he could help paying was well understood ; but that understanding made no difference. Ere long he would be up in the world again, and accordingly many hands were held out to help him in his ascent.

" Wonderful fellow—shrewd fellow ! No

matter the depth of water into which he is thrown, he is sure to rise and strike out for shore—ay, and get to shore too! By Jove! he is the cleverest little vagabond! No use trying to shut him up in a box. He just waits his time, and then—hey presto!—he is out like a conjuring trick, his pockets full of sovereigns and his head full of schemes."

So ran the comments, which delighted Mr. Katzen, as was natural, seeing they contained precisely the sort of praise he valued.

Had the wisdom of Solomon been attributed to him, he would have deemed it foolishness in comparison with the ability to rig the market or run up stock.

He experienced a keen sense of triumph when his dear friend Victor sent a note round to Mitre Court, asking him to call. Mr. Katzen bore no malice towards the excellent Bernberg, whose astuteness had played its owner false for once; nevertheless, he returned an answer, stating he was too much engaged to get to Alderman's Walk; but he was usually to be found at his office between the hours of one and two.

Punctually at half-past one on the day following, Mr. Bernberg appeared in the best of tempers, in the most conciliatory of moods.

"Well," he began, "and how are you getting on? Making your fortune?"

"That is so likely!" returned Mr. Katzen.

"You will manage to net something satisfactory out of the New Andalusian Loan," said Mr. Bernberg.

For answer, Mr. Katzen merely shrugged his shoulders.

"Come!" expostulated his friend. "Why not be frank with me?"

"Frank!" repeated the Consul, turning out the palms of his hands, as though to say —see the very inside of Katzen. "Am I ever other than frank? If you doubt, however, look at the men who are floating this loan, and ask yourself how much is likely to be left for me."

"They do expect a stiff commission then? I suspected as much."

"Ach, mein Gott, you may well say stiff! However, if my people do not wince, why should I? What makes me feel the thing so

deeply is—take any nasty little bankrupt state
—in debt up to its ears—that has never paid,
and never will, and never can pay a farthing,
and see what per cent. will be charged for
floating that loan. Why, Capel Court would
be fighting to see who should obtain the
privilege at a half, or, maybe, an eighth per
cent."

"*Le premier pas.* You remember? Always the case."

"And a country like New Andalusia," went
on Mr. Katzen, "without an encumbrance on
her revenue, abounding in wealth, which
literally merely wants picking up."

"Why does she not pick it up then?"

"Because she has not the means of doing
so. You cannot develop wealth without
money; even gold mines need capital to
work them—eh, Bernberg?"

"True; and so those excellent persons
who have taken New Andalusia in charge
refused to introduce without a heavy consideration?"

"That is so."

"What a pity you did not come to me. I

am poor myself, but still I do know a few individuals who keep big balances, and are glad
to find legitimate outlets for them."

"Ah! my dear friend, but I do not like to
be troubling you always."

" I suppose New Andalusia really does present a fine opening for investment ?"

" I suppose so; you always said it did;
you ought to be a better authority even
than I."

"You have a good memory. I had forgotten. Those gold mines will yield large
returns to some one yet."

" The New Andalusia soil is as valuable
above ground as it is below."

"What a country it must be !"

" And the capabilities of its land sink into
insignificance when compared with the pro-
ducts of its waters," went on the Consul, as
if they had been singing a part-song.

" Bless me, you don't——'

" Yes, I do," interrupted Mr. Katzen.
" There was one thing you missed, when you
surveyed New Andalusia; you left Gulf
Gitana out of the reckoning."

"Gulf Gitana is not in New Andalusia!"

"It is, though, up to a certain point—the valuable side belongs to us. Go home and open your Gazetteer; then ask any pearl merchant, any coral merchant, any sponge importer, about the Gitana pearls, corals, sponges, and listen to what you will hear."

"Of course I have given but little attention to the subject."

"And it is too late to attend to it now," said Mr. Katzen.

"My dear fellow, I can only repeat that I am sorry you did not come to me in the first instance."

"You might not have seen, as you do now, if I had come," answered the Consul. "Anyhow, whatever you might have done or thought once, it is too late to do or think now."

"The loan is being subscribed for satisfactorily, no doubt?"

"I believe so. I have very little to do with it except in name. A first instalment goes out soon, I hear."

"I wish I had some spare cash," said Mr.

Bernberg, " I might be tempted to speculate in a few bonds."

" Don't be tempted," returned the other ; " you can find far better investments for your money than a poor five per cent."

" Perhaps I can," agreed Mr. Bernberg, struck apparently by the depth and beauty of his friend's idea. " Perhaps I can."

" I am very sure you can," said Mr. Katzen. " By-the-bye, I must not forget that I still keep a little in your debt. I had best give you something now."

" Thank you; money is always useful. You can't say I have dunned you much for it."

" No, you have not dunned me ; it would not have been any use if you had."

" Come, Katzen, confess ; you are coining out of this loan ?"

" Upon my sacred word of honour, no. How should I coin ? Of course I shall expect something for my time and trouble, but beyond that, all the good likely to come to me out of it is indirect. I have irons of my own in the fire."

" Poker, shovel, tongs, as somebody says,"
suggested Mr. Bernberg.

" No—no, just little things that help to
keep the pot boiling. I have had to work
hard to get it to boil at all. Since I came
to London, no time has been so uphill as the
last year."

" It had not proved so, had you listened to
reason."

" It is best not to go over all that old
ground again," and Mr. Katzen took out his
cheque-book and began to write.

" Do you want a clerk ?" asked Mr. Bernberg, as he watched this operation. " I know
a young fellow who would suit you to perfection."

" I have a clerk who suits me to perfection," answered the Consul without looking up.

" How did you get him ?"

" By chance—he was out of a job, and glad
to come to me."

" What is this paragon's name ?"

" Rothsattel."

" Rothsattel !" repeated Mr. Bernberg,

bursting into a nasty laugh. "Which of them?"

"Conrad. Why do you laugh?"

"At the notion of your having one of the Rothsattels."

"Why, do you know them?"

"Know them! Of course I know them. I congratulate you on not having the very biggest rogue in London for a clerk. The three brothers are the three degrees of comparison, big—bigger—biggest. Your man is the first."

"He suits me excellently well."

"I do not doubt it. I do not doubt it at all."

There are times when discretion is truly the better part of valour; and Mr. Katzen, feeling this was one of them, refrained from requesting any explanation of Mr. Bernberg's meaning.

As for that gentleman, he went away quite satisfied Mr. Katzen had found a gold mine on his own account, and was working it satisfactorily, wherein he chanced just then to be mistaken, for although the Consul was doing very well, for him, other people were doing much better. New Andalusia had not yet proved an El Dorado for her enthusiastic admirer. No great amount of money was even passing through his hands; but enough found its way to Mitre Court to make matters very easy for him. He could speculate a little, and he did. Every venture proved fortunate. Luck had not stayed in the old house in Botolph Lane, but followed him up Cheapside.

No counting of shillings now! No necessity for regarding watch, or ring, or studs as articles on which advances might be procured. He had repaid Mrs. Jeffley; he had offered Mr. Brisco his hundred pounds with a profit of ten added, showing him how the profit had been made by a careful system of buying and selling, but not deeming it necessary to add that the money had really never been invested in any better security than his own waistcoat pocket.

New Andalusia expressed herself as well satisfied with her Consul. No country perhaps was ever so much surprised as that

favoured land when first the suggestion of a
loan reached her shores. In wildest dreams
such a notion had not entered the minds of
her rulers. They were so much astonished
indeed, that their acceptance of Mr. Katzen's
scheme seemed almost cold. They had no
objection, they stated, to a loan.

" I should think not," commented their
Consul ; " they would be simpletons indeed if
they had."

All in the fine summer weather, therefore,
Mr. Katzen was busy as a bee seeking honey.
He gave himself no rest, he grudged no
trouble. He drew out a prospectus at once
plain and convincing ; he worked, as he himself said, like a pack-horse ; but with all his
endeavours, money did not come pouring in as
he had hoped it might. He had got good men
to float the loan—good respectable men who
had characters to lose, and who would not
have connected themselves with anything
disreputable—and yet even their names failed
to draw the British public to any great extent.

Something more needed to be done, and in

the golden summer-time Mr. Katzen considered how he would do it.

One of the New Andalusian officials, a
very great personage, chanced to be in
Europe, and meant on his way home to
make a short stay in London. The Consul
decided to utilize him; nothing venture,
nothing have.

Mr. Katzen had everything to gain, and
very little to lose.

"What we want is notoriety," he considered. "We must get it somehow."

There is many a true word spoken in jest.
When Mr. Katzen confided this want to himself he had not the slightest idea how amply
it would be provided for. Before any very
long time elapsed, the New Andalusian loan
was as notorious as the heart of its projector
could desire. A man never knows what he
can do till he tries. When Mr. Katzen found
out the extent of his own cleverness, and got
the world to recognise it, even Mr. Bernberg
was moved to a reluctant admiration.

CHAPTER XII.

N one of Fortune's wars which was raging about the time Mr. Jeffley lay ill with his attack of quinsy, it chanced that a certain stockbroker, named Perham, came to great grief.

He was not much worse, and he was certainly no better, than many others who found themselves after the battle sound in credit and in purse; but some one must suffer; and in this case Mr. Nicodemus Perham chanced to be the sufferer.

Also his creditors were sufferers. They had not even the poor consolation of bemoaning their fate in his society. Feeling that farewells are often painful, Mr. Perham considerately determined to spare his friends all trouble on that score, and left England without any foolish ceremony of leave-taking.

Before he was declared a defaulter he had gone no one knew whither, leaving everything behind he could not conveniently take away —amongst other items his family, at that time resident in his town house; and a very pretty villa, with lawns sloping to the Thames, where he had been wont to entertain hospitably during the summer of the year and of his own prosperity.

A villa as new as Mr. Perham himself, and also like that gentleman, built mostly for show—large reception-rooms, hall paved with encaustic tiles, windows containing a painful amount of plate-glass, staring conservatory, boat-house roofed as if it had been a pagoda, and painted with as many colours as Joseph's coat ; gardens, yards, stabling, which required, indeed, as the advertisements said, "only to be seen."

In a word, it was a cockney paradise, a place to which it seemed desirable to ask persons, who were worth conciliating, to

dinner. For some inscrutable reason that at
the time seemed no doubt good enough to
Mr. Perham, Mr. Katzen had once been
invited to spend a Sunday afternoon at
Maple Villa—the name by which this Eden
was known—and the German——thought it
a splendid place then. Inside the house
were mirrors and heavy curtains, and the
most expensive and most comfortable furniture
the best upholsterers could supply; while the
dog-cart in which he was driven over to the
station after a good dinner, a good smoke,
and some excellent wine, was so well ap-
pointed that he hesitated a little before
offering the groom a shilling.

And now Mr. Perham had gone the way a
good deal of seemingly prosperous business
flesh eventually does go, and Maple Villa
knew its former occupier no more.

It was never likely either to know him any
more again for ever. Mr. Perham could not be
found or heard of—himself was an absentee,
his estate in bankruptcy, and his assets, such
as they were, in the hands of a certain firm
of accountants, who meant to go on squeezing

the sponge till not a drop remained in it to reward their exertions.

Mr. Perham had taken such remarkably good care of number one, however, that the sponge-squeezing process proved less satisfactory than might have been hoped.

" He was very selfish, I am afraid," said the trustee, naturally indignant at the thought of such a failing. " Never considered any person but himself. So long as a thing was likely to last his time, it mattered not a row of pins how those fared who were to come after. For example, who but he would have taken that Maple Villa on so short a term ? Had it been freehold now, or even ninety-nine years ; but just the mere fag-end of a lease, what can we do with it ?"

It is mere justice to the speaker to add he tried to dispose of the house and contents as they stood, but failed, and he was about making up his mind to put the furniture up to auction when Mr. Katzen made an offer to rent the residence for the rest of the summer.

There was a little humming and hawing

about the matter. The trustees did not know whether they could so let ; they did not see their way ; they were not quite sure of their position ; but when Mr. Katzen stated his willingness to pay an amount worth while putting in their pockets, and of paying it, moreover, in advance, the speed with which they knew and saw and became satisfied was little short of miraculous.

" Now," thought Mr. Katzen, " we'll give that loan a little shove—it shan't stick, as it is doing, for want of my putting my shoulder to the wheel."

It must have been delightful to the stately gentleman from New Andalusia to see how heartily the Consul threw himself into the scheme for improving the finances of that favoured land.

As some tradesmen have a map showing how every thoroughfare in London has no other end or aim than to lead to their establishments, so Mr. Katzen had his map to prove that all the world's traffic must eventually be conducted to or from New Andalusia. With every prospectus he sent this pictorial

representation of the hitherto neglected resources of that country—too little known.
The railways which were to be, he traced in
red lines, the rivers in blue, connecting canals
in green, new roads in black, towns that as
yet had no existence in yellow; the reference notes on the margin were copious as a
good sized index, while the explanatory
pamphlet compiled by Mr. Katzen, which
accompanied the prospectus, was as lengthy
as a sermon.

The Consul utilized this pamphlet with
great skill. He got it reviewed and noticed
in twenty different ways. In some of the
daily papers he even managed to secure
leaders; in one, New Andalusia was pointed
to as the source England might best look to
for her future supplies of meat; in another,
allusion was made to the inviting field it
offered for emigration. The fathers of large
families were entreated to consider the
promise of a land which merely needed to be
tickled in order to produce waving grain and
the finest of fruits; young men unable to procure employment in England were advised to

secure passages for a country where fortunes awaited enterprise and industry.

The treasures of the deep were dragged up into the light of day; wonderful accounts also were given of cities lying in ruins, concerning which history contained no record—cities built by the nameless dead, and inhabited now merely by wild beasts.

Fortunately, about the same time a volume of travels happened to be published, one portion of which described New Andalusia in glowing terms as a heaven for sportsmen. Its climate was extolled, its inhabitants lauded, the beauty of its scenery spoken of with enthusiasm, its horses represented as the finest in the world.

Mr. Katzen got hold of the author and induced him to give a series of lectures, which paid a great deal better than the book. Little by little, by mere dint of assurance and piling statement upon statement, New Andalusia became for a season as well-known as the Monument.

Each year sees one craze, at all events, possessing the British public; and that year

many persons went crazy about New Andalusia.

" In its sun, in its soil, in its climate, thrice
blessed," quoted the prospectus ; and the
man did not live who could gainsay the truth
of this assertion.

Mr. Katzen had got a good thing, and he
found himself competent to work it.   When
once he warmed thoroughly to his work, he
felt it almost too easy.   With a safe conscience he was able to invite investigation.

Even to Mr. Bernberg's mines he had not
to tell an untruth about anything.   Gold was
in New Andalusia ; how much or how little
scarcely affected the question.   As for the
government, it honestly intended to spend
greater part of the loan in opening up the
country.   Not a penny piece did they owe—
—perhaps for a sufficient reason.   There
were no old scandals that could be raked up,
no cheated creditors to sneer or warn ; all
was fair and above-board—pearls, coral-reefs,
sponges, cattle, game, gold, fertility ; any in-
tending bondholder might satisfy himself
there was no deception.

As is usual in such cases, a cloud of witnesses arose to give testimony concerning the richness of this new land of Goshen. All it required was DEVELOPMENT, and Mr. Katzen evidently meant it should not long lack the means of developing.

He had pretty nearly *carte blanche* to do what he liked. To New Andalusia the idea of getting a loan seemed so utterly amazing, she was prepared to pay heavily for the privilege. She was willing to concede almost anything except the money ; indeed there was nothing she wanted much more than settlers possessed of means and enterprise.

She was quite rejoiced to hear that capitalists were prepared to search her mines, and kill her cattle, and work her fisheries, and cultivate her land, and, if occasionally she did wonder whether there was nothing left in Britain on which to expend its surplus wealth, she was far too lazy to pursue the question to an end.

Anybody who liked to pay for them was welcome to her pearls, or her minerals, or her cattle, or all she possessed, in fact. Payment was essential, but as yet she had not grown extravagant in her ideas.

"That is to come," said Mr. Katzen, laughing. "Happy, in this case, are the first served."

For it was clearly understood that so much per cent. represented but a little of the interest bondholders might look to receive. Figuratively speaking, the whole of New Andalusia was to be at their beck and call. If they found enough money, they might go in and possess.

They would be allowed to fence in the happy hunting-grounds where the buffalo, in a sort of armed neutrality, cropped with the wild cattle; they could plant, and build, and fish, and shoot, and erect meat-preserving sheds, and run out wharves, and, in fact, convert the land of promise into another Albion.

Happy, happy New Andalusia—unlimited gin, unlimited poverty, unlimited ugliness— no wonder your heart waxed warm and your fair face cheerful at such a prospect.

If over your hills a fresh generation of

cattle is now roaming, if in your mines the gold still remains hidden, if your pearls and coral and sponges have not yet drugged the European market, it is scarcely your fault.

When your story comes to be written and your people clad, Moore's line may probably be quoted :

" 'Twas fate, they'll say, a wayward fate ;"

only for fate the name of Katzen may be substituted ; and yet Mr. Katzen worked indefatigably. First and last he garnered something near three hundred thousand pounds, which, however, can be only regarded as a flea-bite in comparison with what New Andalusia wanted.

At Maple Villa the Consul received all sorts and conditions of men. He did not live there—the suburbs or the country, without plenty of society, in fact, represented to him the desolation of abomination. In the abstract he might love nature ; in the concrete he adored the city. In all the world there seemed to him no place so desirable as that tract of pavement round and about the Royal Exchange : and for this reason he only used Maple Villa as a house of entertainment where he invited men who could, he believed, prove useful—men he wanted to impress or humbug.

In this species of commercial diversion he found Mr. Rothsattel an invaluable assistant. He engaged cooks and waiters; he knew how to cater well and yet economically—where to procure the best wines, the oldest brandy, the finest liqueurs. Mr. Katzen had but to say how many guests were to be "victualled," and he was able to dismiss the subject from his mind, confident when the day and the hour arrived everything would be in perfect order.

And so the game went merrily on ; bonds at Mitre Court were dealt out as quietly and swiftly as a pack of cards.

Never before had so much money passed through Mr. Katzen's hands. He disbursed freely, yet prudently. The fame of his doings was wafted across the ocean to New Andalusia, where those in authority congratulated each his fellow upon the cleverness of their Consul.

Through all, however, Mr. Katzen kept himself from being uplifted. He walked with outward serenity through prosperity, as he had walked with apparent calmness while luck kept dead against him.

He did not lose his head and begin to talk big and make enemies—even to Mr. Bernberg he gave himself no airs, though when he happened one day casually to remark he only hoped to get bread and cheese out of the loan, his dear Victor laughed aloud.

" You have a pocket full of concessions, I suppose ?" said that gentleman.

In answer to which Mr. Katzen only shrugged his shoulders.

Everything considered, his humility was really wonderful. He went in and out of Fowkes' Buildings, as Mrs. Jeffley declared, " just like anybody else."

He seemed perfectly contented with its former accommodation, and he did not talk much about Maple Villa, though he once seduced Mr. Jeffley down to look at that desirable residence, which impressed Jack more perhaps than it ought to have done.

" My conscience !" he remarked to Frank Scott after he had described the beauties and glories of Mr. Perham's former abode. " Katzen must be a cleverer fellow than I ever gave him credit for ; why, the place is fit for a lord !"

" Hang him !" That was all Mr. Frank said ; but he said it with fervour.

Mr. Jeffley looked at the young man in a sort of troubled surprise.

" Why, Scott," he exclaimed, " what has come to you ? I used to be bad enough about Katzen—I never did like him, and I never shall ; but you are worse now than I ever was. Seems to me you're altogether changed, man, somehow ; you've never been the same since that night we went up to Mr. Fulmer's."

" Have I not ?" said Frank a little consciously.

" No, and I can't make it out, Frank. You were all for peace and goodwill, and thinking the best of everybody ; but now if you are able to find a nasty thing to say, you say it. What has gone wrong with you, my lad ? Make a clean breast of the trouble."

"I am unhappy," was the reply, "and nobody is genial when unhappy."

"Is that so?" asked Jack; and he considered this proposition while young Scott held his peace.

"I don't quite go with you," went on Mr. Jeffley after a pause; "but that is neither here nor there perhaps. What is more to the purpose, why are you unhappy? Out with the worry—a sorrow told is a sorrow lightened, remember."

"I can tell you no more about it."

"Won't you let me try to help you?"

"No one can help me."

"Well, if you are sure of that——"

"I am quite sure of that."

Mr. Jeffley smoked on in silence; at last he took his pipe from his mouth, knocked out the ashes, and said: "There is one thing, Scott, I think I am sure of too. I am afraid you have got the nineteenth-century complaint."

"I do not understand you."

"The complaint of this part of the nineteenth century anyhow," proceeded Jack slowly—"discontent."

" Do you think I am discontented ?"

" Positive you are ; and how you come to be discontented baffles me.   Eighteen months ago, a brighter, cheerier young fellow couldn't be found ; then you had but a poor salary and no prospects, now you have a fair salary and good prospects."

" No, I have not," interrupted Frank.   " I can see the lie of the country pretty well—I am to work up a business for my principals, and then when I have done it, in will step the two young men, and I may go and hang myself."

Mr. Jeffley looked at the speaker in blank astonishment.

" If that isn't something !" he ejaculated at last.

" I would rather be working for myself in the poorest way," went on Frank vehemently, "than be at the beck and call of any man even at a large salary."

" All alike—all alike !" exclaimed Mr. Jeffley.   " Every servant wants to be master nowadays."

" Surely you cannot blame the servant for that," said Frank.

"Oh! I blame nobody," returned Jack, commencing to fill his pipe once again.

"But you do," was the answer: "you think everybody should be content going on plodding—that he never ought to try to rise."

"I think if a person takes a salary he ought to be satisfied to do the work he takes it for. I can't believe any man can put his heart into his employer's business while he is considering how he can better himself; it isn't feasible, my boy. Maybe with these new lights of yours you'll think I am talking rubbish, but it is right to be single minded. If a man can't serve God and Mammon, and we know that is so, I am very sure he cannot serve his master who pays him weekly or monthly wages, and some tempting speculation in the next street."

Frank Scott looked at Mr. Jeffley with surprised bewilderment, then he said:

"So you imagine speculation is what tempts me?"

"I don't know about speculation," answered Jack; "but I have a suspicion you want to make money too fast."

" No, no—not too fast ; I only want to make it before youth has gone, and hope grown old."

" Stuff !" and Mr. Jeffley smoked calmly on.

" If you knew," began Frank, after a long pause—" if you only could know the hopes with which I came back to England—the purposes I had——"

" Most folks have had hopes and purposes, I suppose," commented Mr. Jeffley drily. " You are not the only one in the world who has fancied he was awake while he was really dreaming. We have all our notions—I know I had mine ; but there—Lord !—what's the use of notions, when people have to earn their bread ?"

Had this been a general proposition, Mr. Francis Scott would have answered, " They are of no use," but when it came to be applied to himself, the complexion of affairs changed. As for Jack, and whatever notions he might ever have indulged in, that also was quite another matter.

Looking at that satisfied, comfortable, unsentimental face, Frank felt his feelings

were one thing, and Mr. Jeffley's another.
Then it flashed upon him there had been a
time when he had thought otherwise; a time
when, without sign or speech, he pitied Jack,
knowing that in his life there was a great
want.

Now—how was it? Had Jack grown
even more commonplace than of yore—or
had he, Frank, gone on? He did not look
at Jack with quite the same eyes as formerly,
and Jack most certainly did not regard him
from exactly the same point of view.

He and Jack had somehow grown apart.
It was very hard indeed, Frank considered,
for he was sure he felt just the same towards
Jack, while Jack knew he was not the same.

And Messrs. Deedes' manager mourned
over the fact with a most unselfish sorrow.
It grieved him to see what he considered the
canker of discontent destroying a nature he
formerly believed sweet; further, he imagined
Frank's recent unsettledness was doing him
no good in St. Dunstan's Hill.

" He got a grand chance, and he is pitching
it away as a child might a diamond," he

thought; "and yet I am half afraid to give
him a hint Deedes' are not altogether pleased,
lest I may make matters worse."

"Look here, Scott," he said at last, breaking
the silence which had followed his last remark,
"whatever hopes you came back to England
with, try to put them behind you. I am vexed
things have not turned out as you wished,
but it is the common lot."

"That is not much comfort," commented
Mr. Scott.

"I think it ought to be," answered Jack.
"It would scarce be pleasant to feel you
had all the world's troubles on your own
shoulders; but whatever you may think about
that, I am very sure you had best make a
clean sweep—wipe the slate and begin a fresh
score—you'll feel ever so much lighter.
What can't be cured, you know, must be
endured."

"You know nothing about what is the
matter with me," returned Frank.

"How should I, when you won't tell me?
What I do know is that you are doing yourself
no good with your employers. Mr. Deedes sees

your heart is not in your work. He has said as much to me. He spoke about you very kindly—but——"

" It was not Mr. Fulmer then ?" interrupted the young man. "I thought perhaps your friend might have been making some remarks on the subject."

" He did not make any remark except that he suspected what was the matter with you."

" Oh ! and what does he suspect ?"

" That you are in love—don't look so angry—he was not finding any fault, he only said he would rather, on the whole, you had taken to drink."

" How kind—how considerate ! He didn't by any chance say who I was in love with ?"

" No ! I made so free as to ask him."

" Is it possible ? And he did not order you out for instant execution ?"

" He only said if he knew, it would not be fair to tell."

" I wish Mr. Fulmer was——" well, what Mr. Frank Scott wished did not sound nice at all.

" Tut-tut-tut," cried Mr. Jeffley. " Frank,

you are set on ruining yourself. I would not have told you a word of all this if I had not felt sure you are trying the firm over-much. They will bear a good deal—but I am in awful fear they may lose patience some fine day, and say what you won't much like to hear."

"But for one thing I would save them the trouble," retorted Mr. Scott, flinging himself in a gust of passion out of the room.

"There," remarked Jack, "I said I would only make matters worse—and I have done it."

BILLING AND SONS, PRINTERS, GUILDFORD.

C. C. & Co.